"I have a proposition for you..."

"How do you feel about marriage?" Jack asked as they cruised down the vacant two-lane headed toward Whitehorse, Montana.

"Marriage?"

Jack grinned, oozing cowboy charm. He was good and all too sexy.

"What do you get out of it?" Josey asked, wary.

"Your company as well as a diversion," Jack said. "You'd be doing me a huge favor and I'd make it worth your while. The ranch is sixty miles from the nearest town and a good twenty from the nearest neighbor."

A remote ranch. Could she really get this lucky? This stranger was offering her exactly what she needed as if he knew how desperate she was. Was it that obvious?

"One week," she said, hoping she wasn't making a huge mistake. Jack had showed up just when she needed him and this marriage charade. No wonder she was feeling this was too good to be true.

But given her lack of options she would rather be the new, *alive,* pretend Mrs. Jack Winchester than the late one.

B.J. DANIELS

HITCHED!

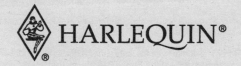

HARLEQUIN®

TORONTO • NEW YORK • LONDON
AMSTERDAM • PARIS • SYDNEY • HAMBURG
STOCKHOLM • ATHENS • TOKYO • MILAN • MADRID
PRAGUE • WARSAW • BUDAPEST • AUCKLAND

This one is for E-Dub. You are always an inspiration!

Recycling programs
for this product may
not exist in your area.

ISBN-13: 978-0-373-69471-6

HITCHED!

Copyright © 2010 by Barbara Heinlein

This edition published by arrangement with Harlequin Books S.A.

For questions and comments about the quality of this book please contact us at Customer_eCare@Harlequin.ca.

www.eHarlequin.com

Printed in U.S.A.

ABOUT THE AUTHOR

B.J. Daniels wrote her first book after a career as an award-winning newspaper journalist and author of thirty-seven published short stories. That first book, *Odd Man Out,* received a four-and-a-half-star review from *RT Book Reviews* and went on to be nominated for Best Intrigue for that year. Since then she has won numerous awards, including a career achievement award for romantic suspense and many nominations and awards for best book.

Daniels lives in Montana with her husband, Parker, and two springer spaniels, Spot and Jem. When she isn't writing, she snowboards, camps, boats and plays tennis. Daniels is a member of Mystery Writers of America, Sisters in Crime, International Thriller Writers, Kiss of Death and Romance Writers of America.

To contact her, write to B.J. Daniels, P.O. Box 1173, Malta, MT 59538 or e-mail her at bjdaniels@mtintouch.net. Check out her Web page at www.bjdaniels.com.

Books by B.J. Daniels

HARLEQUIN INTRIGUE
 996—SECRET OF DEADMAN'S COULEE†
1002—THE NEW DEPUTY IN TOWN†
1024—THE MYSTERY MAN OF WHITEHORSE†
1030—CLASSIFIED CHRISTMAS†
1053—MATCHMAKING WITH A MISSION†
1059—SECOND CHANCE COWBOY†
1083—MONTANA ROYALTY†
1125—SHOTGUN BRIDE*
1131—HUNTING DOWN THE HORSEMAN*
1137—BIG SKY DYNASTY*
1155—SMOKIN' SIX-SHOOTER*
1161—ONE HOT FORTY-FIVE*
1198—GUN-SHY BRIDE**
1204—HITCHED!**

†Whitehorse, Montana
*Whitehorse, Montana: The Corbetts
**Whitehorse, Montana: Winchester Ranch

CAST OF CHARACTERS

Jack Winchester—The grandson of the reclusive Pepper Winchester has come back to the ranch, but not for the reason his grandmother thinks.

Josephine "Josie" Vanderliner—She is on the run when Jack Winchester picks her up beside the road in the middle of nowhere.

Ray Allen "RJ" Evans, Jr.—He saw a way to have it all and made only one mistake when he let Josie get away.

Pepper Winchester—After twenty-seven years, why is the reclusive matriarch of the family inviting her grandchildren back to the ranch?

Sheriff McCall Winchester—The acting sheriff knows her grandmother is up to something as one grandson after another returns to the ranch.

Trace Winchester—His memory still haunts more than the hills around Whitehorse.

Enid Hoagland—The disagreeable gatekeeper at Winchester Ranch has her own reasons for not wanting the family back on the ranch.

Alfred Hoagland—Enid's husband is the silent type, and everyone knows about still waters running deep with dark secrets.

Chapter One

Jack hadn't seen another person in miles when he spotted the woman beside the road. He was cruising along Highway 191, headed north through the most unpopulated part of Montana, when he saw her.

At first he blinked, convinced she had to be a mirage, since he hadn't even seen another car in hours. But there she was, standing beside the road, hip cocked, thumb out, a mane of long, ginger hair falling past her shoulders, blue jeans snug-fitting from her perfect behind down her impossibly long legs.

Jack slowed, already having doubts before he stopped next to her in his vintage, pale yellow Cadillac convertible. Just the sight of her kicked up the heat on an already warm May day.

She had a face that would make any man look twice. He watched her take in the restored convertible first then sweep her green-eyed gaze over him. He thought of warm, tropical sea breezes.

Until he looked closer. As warm as the day was, she wore a jean jacket, the collar turned up. He caught a glimpse of a stained T-shirt underneath. Her sneakers looked wet, like her hair. Her clothes were dusty and the cuffs of her jeans wet and muddy.

He'd seen an empty campground in the cottonwoods as he passed the Missouri River, but it was still early in this part of Montana to be camping, since the nights would be cold. It was especially too early to be bathing in the river, but he had to assume that was exactly what she'd done.

"Going any place in particular?" he asked, worried what she was doing out here in the middle of nowhere all alone. Assuming that was the case. He glanced toward the silky-green pine trees lining the road, half-expecting her boyfriend to come barreling out of them at any minute. But then, that was the way his suspicious mind worked.

"Up the highway." She leaned down to pick up the dirty backpack at her feet. It appeared as road worn as she was.

All Jack's instincts told him he'd regret giving this woman a ride. But it was what he glimpsed in her eyes that made up his mind. A little fear was normal for a woman traveling alone in the middle of nowhere. This woman was terrified of something.

He saw her glance back down the highway toward the river, that terror glittering in all that green.

"Then I guess you're going my way." He smiled, wondering what the hell this woman was running from and why he was opening himself up to it. Any fool knew that a woman on the run had trouble close at her heels. "Hop in."

She swung the backpack to her shoulder, straightened the collar of her jean jacket and shot another look back down the lonesome highway.

Jack glanced in his rearview, half-afraid of what had her so scared. Heat rose from the empty two-lane blacktop. He caught a glimpse of the river below them, the dark surface glistening in the morning sunlight. A hawk squawked as it soared on a current coming up out of the river. A cloud passed overhead, throwing the rugged ravines and gullies choked with scrub juniper and pine into shadow.

As he turned back, she was apologizing for her muddy sneakers.

"Don't worry about that," he said, figuring this woman had a lot more to worry about than getting his car dirty.

As he reached across to open her door, she dropped her backpack onto the passenger-side floorboard and slid into the seat, closing the door behind her.

Jack tried to shove off his second thoughts about picking up a total stranger on the run from beside the road in such a remote, isolated place as he watched her settle into the soft leather.

He couldn't miss the way she pulled her bulging backpack protectively between her feet. The backpack, like her T-shirt, was stained with dirt and splattered with something dark the color of dried blood.

"Name's Jack. Jack Winchester." Then he asked, "I'm on my way to the Winchester Ranch. You don't happen to know the Winchesters, do you?"

"I don't know a living soul in Montana." She took his outstretched hand. Her skin was silky smooth and just as cool. "Josey." Her eyes widened a little, as if that had just slipped out. "Josey Smith."

She'd stumbled on the last name, a clear lie. It made him wonder again who or what was after her. "Nice to meet you, Josey." He told himself he was just giving her a ride up the road as far as the turnoff to the ranch.

Shifting the Caddie into gear, he took off. As they

topped the mountain and left the river and wild country of the Breaks behind, he saw her take one last look back. But the fear didn't leave her eyes as they roared down the long, empty highway.

JOSEY FOUGHT to still the frantic pounding of her heart. She didn't want this man to see how desperate she was. She was still shaking inside as she turned up the collar on her jean jacket and lay back against the seat.

She needed time to think. It still wasn't clear to her what had happened back there on the river.

Liar. She closed her eyes, trying to block it all out. But the memory was too fresh. Just like the pain. She could still see the car breaking the dark green surface and sinking, hear the gurgling sound as water rushed in, see the huge bubbles that boiled to the surface.

She'd stumbled and fallen as she scaled the rocky bluff over the river, then worked her way through the pines, not daring to look back. She'd only just broken out of the trees and onto the highway when she'd heard the growl of an engine and spotted the Cadillac coming up the hill. It was the first vehicle she'd seen or heard in hours.

Holding her breath and reining in her urge to run, she'd stuck out her thumb—and prayed. Her only hope was to get as far away as she could. She'd been scared the driver of the Cadillac wouldn't stop for her. She could just imagine the way she looked.

But he had stopped, she thought. That alone made her wary. She tried to concentrate on the warm spring breeze on her face, telling herself she was alive. It seemed a miracle. She'd gotten away. She was still shaking, though, still terrified after the horror of the past two days.

She opened her eyes, fighting the urge to look back down the highway again, and glanced over at the man who'd picked her up. Under normal circumstances she would have thought twice about getting into a car with a complete stranger, especially out here where there were no houses, no people, nothing but miles and miles of nothing.

Jack Winchester looked like a rancher in his jeans, boots, and fancy Western shirt. His dark blond hair curled at his nape under the black Stetson. She glanced down at her own clothing and cringed. She looked as if she'd been wallowing in the dirt. She had.

Furtively, she brushed at her jeans and, unable to refrain any longer, turned to look back down the highway.

Empty.

She felt tears sting her eyes. He wasn't coming after her. He couldn't ever hurt her again. She shuddered at the thought.

Not that it was over. By now California criminal investigators would have put out an all-points bulletin on her. Before long she'd be wanted in all fifty states for murder—and they didn't know the half of it.

AHEAD, THE LITTLE ROCKIES were etched purple against the clear blue sky of the spring day. As the land changed from the deep ravines and rocky ridges of the Missouri Breaks to the rolling prairie, Jack watched his passenger out of the corner of his eye. She chewed at her lower lip, stealing glances in the side mirror at the highway behind them. She had him looking back, as well.

Fortunately, the two-lane was empty.

As he neared the turnoff to the ranch, Jack realized he couldn't just put her out beside the road. He couldn't imagine how she came to be hitchhiking, but his every instinct told him she was in danger.

He could only assume it was from some man she'd hooked up with and later regretted. Whoever was after her, Jack didn't want him or her to catch up with his passenger.

He knew it was crazy. The last thing he needed was to get involved in this woman's problems. But he also didn't want her blood on his hands.

A thought crossed his mind. He prided himself at thinking on his feet. Also at using situations to his advantage.

And it appeared fate had literally dropped this woman into his lap. Or at least dropped her into his Caddie. Josey couldn't have been more perfect if he'd ordered her from a catalog. The more he thought about it, the more he liked his idea, and he wondered why he hadn't thought of it before he'd agreed to this visit to the "family" ranch.

He glanced over at her. She had her eyes closed again, her head back, her hair blowing behind her in a tangled wave of sun-kissed copper. She was stunning, but beyond that his instincts told him that this woman wasn't the type who normally found herself in this kind of position beside a road, and possibly running for her life.

Jack reminded himself that his instincts had also warned him not to pick her up back there.

He smiled to himself. Taking chances was nothing new to him, nor was charming his way to what he wanted. He'd been told that he could talk a rattlesnake out of its venom without even a bite. He knew he could talk this woman into what he had in mind or his name wasn't Jack Winchester.

But he didn't figure it would take much charming. He had a feeling she'd go for his proposal because she needed this more than he did.

"So, Josey, how do you feel about marriage?" he asked as they cruised down the vacant two-lane headed toward Whitehorse, Montana.

"Marriage?" she asked, opening one eye.

Jack grinned. "I have a proposition for you."

Chapter Two

Josey had been taken aback, instantly suspicious until he explained that he was on his way to see his grandmother, who was in her seventies.

"She has more money than she knows what to do with and lives on a huge ranch to the east of here," Jack said. "You'd be doing me a huge favor, and I'd make it worth your while. The ranch is sixty miles from the nearest town and a good ten from the nearest neighbor."

A remote ranch. Could she really get this lucky? He was offering her exactly what she needed, as if he knew how desperate she was. Was it that obvious?

"What do you get out of it?" she asked, wary.

"Your company as well as a diversion. Since we're on our honeymoon I have the perfect excuse to spend less time at my grandmother's bedside."

"I take it you aren't close."

He laughed at that. "You have no idea."

Still, she made him work for it. This wasn't her first rodeo, as they said out here in the West, and Jack Winchester was definitely not the first con man she'd come across in her twenty-eight years.

He was good, though, smooth, sexy and charming as the devil, with a grin that would have had her naked—had she still been young and naive.

She was neither. She'd learned the hard way about men like Jack Winchester back in her wild days.

But she also knew he would be suspicious if she gave in right away.

"One week," she said, hoping she wasn't making a huge mistake. Jack had showed up just when she needed him and this marriage charade. No wonder she was feeling this was too good to be true.

But given her lack of options...

He flashed her a sexy grin, and she told herself all she had to do was resist his cowboy charm for a week. No problem.

She closed her eyes and dozed until she felt him slowing down on the outskirts of what appeared to be a small Western town nestled in a river bottom.

"Welcome to Whitehorse," Jack said with a laugh as they crossed a narrow bridge. "I thought we'd buy a few things for you to wear this week. I'm guessing you don't have a lot of clothing in that backpack."

That almost made her laugh as she pulled the backpack closer. "I definitely could use some clothes and a shower before I meet your grandmother."

"No problem. Just tell me what you need. I'm sure there's a truck stop at one end of this town or another. It's the only town for miles up here."

She looked over at him. He was making this too easy. Was he thinking that with a wife his grandmother would give him twice the inheritance? "You're sure about this? Because I'm really not dressed to go into a clothing store," she said, sliding down in the seat as they entered town.

JACK FELT A CHILL as Josey turned up the collar on her jean jacket and slid down in her seat. *Who the hell is after her? And what the hell have I got myself into?*

Still, the gambler in him told him to stick to his plan. He couldn't throw this woman to the wolves. "My wife can have anything she wants or needs," he said. "Just name it."

And she did, including hair dye and a pair of sharp scissors. He hadn't even lifted a brow, but he'd hated the thought of what she planned to do to that beautiful hair of hers.

It definitely brought home the realization that he'd underestimated just how much trouble this woman was in. "I'll tell you what. Why don't I drop you at the truck stop? You can get a hot shower, get out of those clothes and I'll come by with everything else you need."

"You don't know my size."

"I'm good at guessing." He saw her hesitate. "Trust me."

Like a dog that'd been kicked too many times, her look said, *When hell freezes over.*

She told him what else she needed, which turned out to be just about everything. He had to wonder what *was* in that backpack. It looked full. But apparently there wasn't much clothing in it.

Whatever was in the backpack, it was something she wasn't letting out of her sight. She kept the backpack close, taking it with her when he dropped her at the truck stop.

Jack watched her walk away, her head down as if trying to go unnoticed, and told himself he was going to regret this.

JOSEY DIDN'T EXPECT to see Jack Winchester again as he drove away from the truck stop. She wouldn't have blamed him. She'd caught the look that crossed his handsome face when she'd asked for the dark hair dye and scissors.

Only a fool wouldn't get the implication of that and Jack, she suspected, was no fool. By the time she'd showered, she'd found the items she'd asked for waiting for her just outside the shower door.

She took the scissors to her hair, surprised by how painful it was. It was just hair. It would grow back. But she knew she wasn't upset about her hair. It was all the other losses in her life.

She let the dye set in her short hair as she avoided looking in the mirror, then took another shower, wondering if she would ever feel truly clean again. In the bags he'd left for her, she found jeans, shirts, a couple of summer dresses, sandals, undergarments, a robe and nightgown, and even a pair of cowboy boots.

Josey shook her head, amazed that he would make so many purchases including the two scarves she'd asked for. He really was good at guessing. He'd not only guessed her sizes right down to her shoe size, but he'd chosen colors and styles that she might have chosen for herself.

She'd been so touched, it had choked her up, and she realized how long it had been since someone had been nice to her.

Jack was waiting for her in the shade outside beside the Cadillac. It surprised her that she'd been dreading his reaction to the change in her appearance. She'd worn the boots, jeans and Western shirt he'd bought her, as well as a scarf tied around her neck that went with the shirt.

He smiled when he saw her. His gaze took in her hair first, then the rest of her. "I see the clothes fit."

"Yes, thank you." She felt strangely shy.

"I like your new look," he said, nodding, as they climbed into the car.

"You do?" she asked, and braved checking herself in the vanity mirror. It startled her, seeing herself as a brunette with short curly hair that framed her face. Her green eyes appeared huge to her. Or maybe it was the dark shadows under them. She didn't even recognize herself.

"It suits you," he said.

"Thank you." She snapped the visor up. Who was she kidding? Changing her hairstyle wasn't going to save her. Nothing would. It was just a matter of time before the rest of her world came crashing down.

She saw Jack looking at her backpack again, even more curious. She'd put her dirty clothing and sneakers into one of the shopping bags, and had to stuff the second bag with the new clothing.

She'd have to watch him closely until she had an opportunity to hide the backpack's contents for safekeeping during the week at the ranch.

If she lasted the week. If there was even a ranch, she thought, as Jack drove south on a highway even less traveled than the last one they'd been on.

She no longer trusted herself to separate the good guys from the bad.

JACK STUDIED JOSEY as they left town. The new hairstyle and color only made her more striking. A woman like her couldn't go unnoticed, if that was what she was hoping. So far, he thought she was safe. The truck stop hadn't been busy, and the clerk there hadn't given either of them a second glance. She'd been too busy watching the small television behind the counter.

Jack had noticed that when Josey came out to the car she'd carried both bags of clothing he'd purchased for her as well as that backpack she refused to let out of her sight. With her dirty clothes in one bag and the other bag overstuffed with her new clothes, he was even more concerned about what was in her backpack.

"You didn't have to buy me so much," Josey said now as he drove east out of town.

"I wouldn't want my grandmother to think that I'm cheap when it comes to my wife and her wardrobe."

His expression sobered at the thought of his grandmother, Pepper Winchester. He didn't give a damn what she thought, but he *did* want her to believe this marriage was real. It hadn't crossed his mind to bring a "wife" along. Not until he'd picked up Josey beside the road and had this overwhelming desire to help her. *No good deed goes unpunished,* he could hear his father say.

Jack admitted that his motives hadn't been completely selfless. Having a wife would allow him more freedom on the ranch, freedom he would need.

He thought of his mother and told himself he was doing this for her. It wasn't about revenge. It was about justice.

As he glanced over at Josey, he knew he would have to be careful, though. Josey was a beautiful woman. He couldn't afford to get involved in her trouble and lose sight of why he was really going to the ranch.

He reminded himself Josey had gone along with the

"marriage" because she needed to hide out somewhere safe for a week—just as he'd suspected. What was there to worry about?

"I hope we've got everything we need," he said, glancing back at Whitehorse in his rearview mirror. The tiny Western town was only about ten blocks square with more churches than bars, one of the many small towns that had spouted up beside the tracks when the railroad had come through.

"A few more miles and it will be the end of civilization as we know it," Jack said. "There are no convenience stores out here, nothing but rolling prairie as far as the eye can see."

"It sounds wonderful," she said.

"I should probably fill you in on my grandmother," Jack said, as the road turned to gravel and angled to the southeast. "She's been a recluse for the past twenty-seven years and now, according to her attorney, she wants to see her family. The letter I received made it sound as if she is dying."

Josey looked sympathetic. "I'm sorry. A recluse for twenty-seven years? I can understand why you might not have been close."

"I was six the last time I saw her." But he remembered her only too well. Her and the ranch and those long summer days with his mother, all of them living a lie.

As Jack drove out of Whitehorse, Josey felt a little better. She'd been nervous in town, trying hard not to look over her shoulder the whole time. At the truck stop, she'd just about changed her mind. She desperately needed to put more distance between her and her past. But the only other option was hooking a ride with a trucker passing through, since there appeared to be no place in this town that she could rent a car or even buy one.

Also, why chance it when she could hide out for a week at some remote ranch? She was anxious to do the one thing she needed to do, but it would have to wait just a little longer. She certainly couldn't chance walking into a bank in this town. It was too risky.

But then again, how risky was it pretending to be a stranger's wife? Even as desperate as she was. Even as good-looking and normal as Jack Winchester appeared.

Who was this man? And what was the deal with his reclusive grandmother? She reminded herself how bad her judgment had been lately, her hand going to her neck beneath the scarf and making her wince with pain. She hoped she hadn't just jumped from the frying pan into the fire.

As the Cadillac roared down the fairly wide gravel road through rolling grasslands and rocky knolls, she tried to relax. But Jack Winchester had her confused. He seemed like a nice guy, but nice guys didn't fool their grandmothers with fake wives.

Even though she'd fought it, Josey must have dozed off. She woke as the Cadillac hit a bump and sat up, surprised to see that the road they were on had narrowed to a dirt track. The land had changed, becoming more rough, more desolate.

There were no buildings, nothing but wild country, and she had the feeling there hadn't been for miles.

"Is the ranch much farther?" she asked, afraid she'd been duped. Again.

Sagebrush dotted the arid hills and gullies, and

stunted junipers grew along rocky breaks. Dust boiled up behind the Cadillac, the road ahead more of the same.

"It's a bit farther," Jack said. "The ranch isn't far from a paved highway—as the crow flies. But the only way to get there is this road, I'm afraid."

Josey felt a prickle of fear skitter over her skin. *But come on, what man would buy you clothes just to take you out in the middle of nowhere and kill you?* She shuddered, thinking she knew a man exactly like that.

"You thought I was kidding about the Winchester Ranch being remote?" Jack asked with a laugh.

When he had told her about where they would be spending the week, she had thought it perfect. But now she doubted there was even a ranch at the end of this road. It wouldn't be the first time she'd been played for a fool, but it could be the last. Josey had a bad feeling that she'd used up any luck she'd ever had a long time ago.

She shifted in her seat and drew the backpack closer, considering what she was going to do if this turned out to be another trap. Jack didn't look like a deranged madman who was driving all this way to torture and kill her. But then RJ hadn't looked like a deranged madman, either, had he?

She stared at the road ahead as Jack drove deeper into the wild, uninhabited country. Occasionally she would see a wheat field, but no sign of a house or another person.

As the convertible came over a rise in the road, Jack touched his brakes, even though all she could see was more of the same wild landscape. He turned onto an even less used road, the land suddenly dropping precariously.

"Are you sure you're on the right road?" Her hand went to her backpack, heart hammering in her chest as she eased open the drawstring and closed her hand around the gun handle, realizing she had only four shots left.

"I'm beginning to wonder about that myself. I asked for directions back at a gas station in town before I picked you up, so I'm pretty sure I'm on the right road." The car bumped down the uneven track, then turned sharply to the right. "There it is." He sounded as relieved as she felt.

Josey looked up in surprise to see a cluster of log buildings at the base of the rugged hills behind it. A little farther down the road Jack turned under a huge weathered wooden arch, with the words *Winchester Ranch* carved in it.

Her relief was almost palpable. Josey released her hold on the pistol, trying to still her thundering heart as the Cadillac bumped down the narrow dirt road toward the ranch buildings.

She frowned, noting suddenly how the grass had grown between the two tracks in the road, as if it hadn't had much use. As they grew closer, she saw that the cluster of log buildings looked old and...deserted.

Josey reminded herself that the grandmother had been a recluse for the past twenty-seven years. At least that was what Jack had said. So she probably hadn't had a lot of company or use on the road.

After what she'd been through, Josey thought she could handle anything. But she suddenly feared that wasn't true. She didn't feel strong enough yet to be tested again. She wasn't sure how much more she could take before she broke.

As they rounded a bend in the road, her pulse quickened. This place was huge and creepy-looking. Sun glinted off a line of bleached white antlers piled in the middle of a rock garden. She noticed other heads of dead animals, the bones picked clean and hanging on the wood fence under a row of huge cottonwoods. As she looked at the house, she thought of the "big bad wolf" fairy tale and wondered if a kindly grandmother—or something a lot more dangerous—was waiting inside.

Jack parked in front and killed the engine. A breathless silence seemed to fill the air. Nothing moved. A horse whinnied from a log barn in the distance, startling Josey. Closer a bug buzzed, sounding like a rattlesnake. She felt jumpy and wondered if she'd lost her mind going along with this.

"Are you all right?" he asked. He looked worried.

She nodded, realizing she was here now and had little choice but to go through with it. But this ranch certainly wasn't what she'd expected. Not this huge, eerie-looking place, that was for sure.

"I know it doesn't look like much," Jack said, as if reading her mind.

The house was a massive, sprawling log structure with wings running off from the main section and two stories on all but one wing that had an odd third story added toward the back. The place reminded her of a smaller version of Old Faithful Lodge in Yellowstone Park.

At one time, the building must have been amazing. But it had seen better days and now just looked dark and deserted, the grimy windows like blind eyes staring blankly out at them.

"Don't look so scared," Jack said under his breath. "My grandmother isn't that bad. Really." He made it sound like a joke, but his words only unnerved her further.

As the front door opened, an elderly woman with long, plaited salt-and-pepper hair filled the doorway. Her braid hung over one shoulder of the black caftan she wore, her face in shadow.

"Showtime," Jack said as he put his arm around Josey and drew her close. She fit against him, and for a moment Josey could almost pretend this wasn't a charade, she was so relieved that at least part of Jack's story had been true. An old woman lived here. Was this the grandmother?

Jack planted a kiss in her hair and whispered, "We're newlyweds, remember." There was a teasing glint in his blue gaze as he dropped his mouth to hers.

The kiss was brief, but unnervingly powerful. As Jack pulled back he frowned. "I can see why we eloped so quickly after meeting each other," he said, his voice rough with a desire that fired his gaze. This handsome man was much more dangerous than she'd thought. In at least one way, she had definitely jumped from the skillet into the fire.

She gave Jack a playful shove as if she'd just seen the woman in the doorway and was embarrassed, then checked to make sure the scarf around her neck was in place before opening her door and stepping out, taking the backpack with her. *Showtime,* she thought, echoing Jack's words.

No one would ever find her here, wherever she was.

She had to pull this off. She was safe. That was all she had to think about right now, and as long as she was safe her mother would be, as well. One week. She could do this.

Jack was by her side in a flash, his arm around her, as they walked toward the house. An ugly old dog came out growling, but the elderly woman shooed him away with her cane.

Josey studied the woman in the doorway as she drew closer. Jack's grandmother? She didn't have his coloring. While he was blond and blue-eyed, she was dark from her hair to her eyes, a striking, statuesque woman with a face that could have been chiseled from marble, it was so cold.

"Hello, Grandmother," Jack said, giving the woman a kiss on her cheek. "This is my wife—"

"Josey Winchester," Josey said, stepping forward and extending her hand. The woman took it with obvious surprise—and irritation. Her hand was ice-cold, and her vapid touch sent a chill through Josey.

"I didn't realize you were married, let alone that you'd be bringing a wife," his grandmother said.

Jack hadn't planned on bringing a wife. So why had he? Josey wondered. It certainly hadn't ingratiated his grandmother to him. And as for money…was there any? This place didn't suggest it.

"This is my grandmother, Pepper Winchester," Jack said, an edge to his voice.

The elderly woman leaned on her cane, her gaze skimming over Josey before shifting back to Jack. "So, you're my son Angus's boy."

Wouldn't she *know* he was her son's child? The

woman must be senile, Josie thought. Or was there some reason to question his paternity?

"I remember the day your mother showed up at the door with you," Pepper said. "What were you then?"

"Two," Jack said, clearly uncomfortable.

His grandmother nodded. "Yes. I should have been suspicious when Angus involved himself in the hiring of the nanny," Pepper said.

So Jack was the bastard grandson. That explained this less than warm reception.

Jack's jaw muscle tensed, but his anger didn't show in his handsome face. He put his arm around Josey's waist and pulled her closer, as if he needed her as a buffer between him and his grandmother. Another reason he'd made her this phony marriage offer?

When he'd told her about his grandmother and this visit, Josey had pictured an elderly woman lying in bed hooked up to machines, about to take her final gasp.

This woman standing before them didn't look anywhere near death's door. Josey had speculated that this was about money. What else? But if she was right, then Jack had underestimated his grandmother. This woman looked like someone who planned to live forever and take whatever she had with her.

"Since I didn't realize you had a wife," Pepper Winchester was saying, "I'll have to instruct my housekeeper to make up a different room for you."

"Please don't go to any trouble on my account," Jack said.

The grandmother smiled at this, cutting her dark gaze to him, eyes narrowing.

Be careful, Josie thought. *This woman is sharp.*

JACK HESITATED at the door to the huge ranch lodge. This place had once been filled with happy memories for him, because he'd lived here oblivious to what was really going on. Ignorance had been bliss. He'd played with the other grandchildren, ridden horses, felt like a Winchester even before his mother had confessed that he was one and he realized so much of their lives had been lies.

"Coming, dear?" Josey called from the open front doorway.

He looked at his beautiful wife and was more than grateful she'd agreed to this. He wasn't sure he could have done it alone. Josey, so far, was a godsend. His grandmother was a lot more on the ball than he'd thought she would be at this age.

Grandma had disappeared into the musty maze of the lodge, leaving them in the entryway. Jack was surprised that he still felt awe, just as he had the first time he'd seen it. This place had been built back in the nineteen forties and had the feel of another era in Western history.

He stared at the varnished log stairway that climbed to the upper floors, remembering all the times he'd seen his mother coming down those stairs.

"Mrs. Winchester said you are to wait down here." Jack swung around, surprised to see the gnarled, petite elderly woman who had managed to sneak up on them. To his shock, he recognized her. "Enid?" She was still alive?

If she recognized him, she gave no indication as she pointed down the hallway then left, saying she had to get their room ready. She left grumbling to herself.

Behind them, the front door opened, and an elderly

man came in carrying Jack's two pieces of luggage from the trunk of the Cadillac. Alfred, Enid's husband. Amazing.

He noticed that Josey still had her backpack slung over one shoulder.

Alfred noticed, as well. "I'll take that," the old man said, pointing to it.

She shook her head, her hand tightening around the strap. "I'll keep it with me, thank you."

Alfred scowled at her before heading up the stairs, his footsteps labored under the weight of the bags and his disapproval.

"I can't believe those two are still alive," Jack whispered to Josey, as he led her down the hallway. "I remember them both being old when I was a kid. I guess they weren't that old, but they sure seemed it." He wondered if his grandmother would be joining them and was relieved to find the parlor empty.

Josey took a seat, setting her backpack on the floor next to her, always within reach. Jack didn't even want to speculate on what might be in it. He had a bad feeling it was something he'd be better off not knowing.

Chapter Three

Deputy Sheriff McCall Winchester had been back to work for only a day when she got a call from a fisherman down at the Fred Robinson Bridge on the Missouri River. Paddlefish season hadn't opened yet. In a few weeks the campground would be full with fishermen lined up along the banks dragging huge hooks through the water in the hopes of snagging one of the incredibly ugly monstrous fish.

This fisherman had been on his way up to Nelson Reservoir, where he'd heard the walleye were biting, but he'd stopped to make a few casts in the Missouri as a break in the long drive, thinking he might hook into a catfish.

Instead he'd snagged a piece of clothing—attached to a body.

"It's a woman," he'd said, clearly shaken. "And she's got a rope around her neck. I'm telling you, it's a damned noose. Someone hung her!"

Now, as McCall squatted next to the body lying on a tarp at the edge of the water, she saw that the victim looked to be in her mid-twenties. She wore a thin cotton top, no bra and a pair of cutoff jeans over a bright red thong that showed above the waist of the cutoffs. Her hair was dyed blond, her eyes were brown and as empty as the sky overhead, and around her neck was a crude noose of sisal rope. A dozen yards of the rope were coiled next to her.

McCall studied the ligature marks around the dead woman's neck as the coroner loosened the noose. "Can you tell if she was dead before she went into the water?"

Coroner George Murphy shook his head. "But I can tell you that someone abused the hell out of her for some time before she went into the water." He pointed to what appeared to be cigarette burns on her thin arms and legs.

"Before he *hung* her."

"What kind of monster does stuff like that?" George, a big, florid-faced man in his early thirties, single and shy, was new to this. As an EMT, he'd gotten the coroner job because Frank Brown had retired and no one else wanted it.

"Sheriff?"

McCall didn't respond at first. She hadn't gotten used to being acting sheriff. Probably because she hadn't wanted the job and suspected there was only one reason she had it—Pepper Winchester.

But when the position opened, no one wanted to fill in until a sheriff could be elected. The other deputies all had families and young children and didn't want the added responsibility.

McCall could appreciate that.

"Sheriff, we found something I think you'd better see."

"Don't tell me you found another body," the coroner said.

McCall turned to see what the deputy was holding. Another noose. Only this one was wrapped around a large tree trunk that the deputies had pulled up onto the riverbank.

As McCall walked over to it, she saw two distinct grooves in the limb where two ropes had been tied. Two ropes. Two nooses. The thick end of the dead branch had recently broken off.

She looked upriver. If the limb had snapped off under the weight of two people hanging from it, then there was a good chance it had fallen into the river and floated down to where the deputy had found it dragging the second noose behind it.

"Better go upriver and see if you can find the spot where our victim was hung," McCall said. "And we better start looking for a second body in the river."

PEPPER WINCHESTER RUBBED her temples as she paced the worn carpet of her bedroom, her cane punctuating her frustration.

The first of her grandchildren had arrived—with a new wife. She shouldn't have been surprised, given Jack's lineage. None of her sons had a lick of sense when it came to women. They were all too much like their father, suffer his soul in hell. So why should her grandsons be any different?

Her oldest son Worth—or Worthless, as his father had called him—had taken off with some tramp he met in town after Pepper had kicked him out. She would imagine he'd been through a rash of ill-conceived relationships since then.

Brand had married another questionable woman and

had two sons, Cordell and Cyrus, before she'd taken off, never to be seen again.

Angus had knocked up the nanny and produced Jack. She shuddered to think how that had all ended.

Trace, her beloved youngest son, had gotten murdered after marrying Ruby Bates and producing McCall, her only granddaughter that she knew of.

Pepper stepped to the window, too restless to sit. When she'd conceived this plan to bring her family back to the ranch, she wasn't sure who would come. She'd thought the bunch of them would be greedy enough or at least curious enough to return to the ranch. She didn't kid herself that none of them gave two cents for her. She didn't blame them, given the way she'd kicked them all off the ranch twenty-seven years ago and hadn't seen one of them since.

So why was she surprised that Jack wasn't what she'd expected? The same could be said for his wife. She wasn't sure what to make of either of them yet.

She pulled back the curtain and stared out at the land. *Her* land. She remembered the first time she'd seen it. She'd been so young and so in love when Call had brought her back here after their whirlwind love affair and impromptu marriage.

He hadn't known any more about her than she had him.

How foolish they both had been.

It had been hard at first, living on such an isolated, remote ranch. Call had hired a staff to do everything and insisted no wife of his would have to lift a finger.

Pepper had been restless. She'd learned to ride a horse and spent most of her days exploring the ranch. That was how she'd met neighboring rancher Hunt McCormick.

She shivered at the memory as she spotted movement in the shadows next to the barn. Squinting, she saw that it was Enid and her husband, Alfred. They had their heads together and their conversation looked serious. It wasn't the first time she'd caught them like that recently.

What were they up to? Pepper felt her stomach roil. As if her family wasn't worry enough.

JOSEY STUDIED JACK. He seemed nervous now that they were here at the ranch. Was he realizing, like her, that his grandmother had gotten him here under false pretenses?

"As you've probably gathered, my mother was the nanny here as well as the mistress of Angus Winchester, my father," Jack said distractedly, as he moved to look out the window. "According to my mother, they had to keep their affair secret because my grandmother didn't approve and would have cut Angus off without a cent." He turned to look at her. "As it was, Pepper cut him and the rest of her family off twenty-seven years ago without a cent, saying she didn't give a damn what they did. When my father died, my grandmother didn't even bother to come to his funeral or send flowers or even a card."

"Why would you come back here to see your grandmother after that?" Josey had to ask.

He laughed at her outraged expression. "There is no one quite like Pepper Winchester. It wasn't just me, the bastard grandson, she washed her hands of after her youngest son disappeared. Trace Winchester was her life. She couldn't have cared less about the rest of her offspring, so I try not to take it personally."

Shocked, she watched Jack study an old photograph on the wall. "If the only reason you came here is because you thought she was dying—"

"It isn't the only reason, although I've been hearing about the Winchester fortune as far back as I can remember." Jack smiled as he glanced at her over his shoulder. "She looks healthy as a horse, huh? I wonder what she's up to and where the others are."

"The others?" she asked.

"My grandmother had five children. Virginia, the oldest, then Worth, Angus, Brand and Trace."

"You haven't mentioned your grandfather."

"Call Winchester? According to the story Pepper told, he rode off on a horse about forty years ago. His horse came back but Call never did. There was speculation he'd just kept riding, taking the opportunity to get away from my grandmother."

Josey could see how that might be possible.

"When Trace disappeared twenty-seven years ago, it looked like he was taking a powder just like his father," Jack said. "I would imagine that's what pushed my grandmother over the edge, and why she locked herself up in this place all the years since."

"So what changed?"

"Trace Winchester's remains were found buried not far from here. Apparently he was murdered, and that's why no one had seen him the past twenty-seven years."

"Murdered?"

"Not long after his remains were found I got a letter from my grandmother's attorney saying my grandmother wanted to see me." Jack walked over to the window again and pushed aside the dark, thick drape. Dust motes danced in the air. "It was more of a summons than an invitation. I guess I wanted to see what the old gal was up to. Pepper Winchester never does anything without a motive."

His grandmother had suffered such loss in her lifetime. To lose her husband, then her youngest son? Josey couldn't even imagine what that would do to a person. She could also understand how Jack would be bitter and angry, but it was the underlying pain in Jack that made her hurt for him. She knew only too well the pain family could inflict.

The last thing she wanted, though, was to feel anything for Jack Winchester.

Nor did she want to get involved in his family drama. She had her own problems, she reminded herself. She pulled her backpack closer, then with a start realized there was someone standing in the doorway.

The housekeeper Jack had called Enid. Josey wondered how long the woman had been standing there listening. She was one of those wiry old women with a scornful face and small, close-set, resentful eyes.

Enid cleared her throat. "If you'll come with me." She let out a put-upon sigh before leading them back to the staircase.

As they climbed, Josey took in the antique furniture, the rich tapestries, the thick oriental rugs and the expensive light fixtures. She tried to estimate what some of the pieces might be worth. Maybe there was money here—if the ranch wasn't mortgaged to the hilt. She feared that whatever had brought Jack here, he was going to be disappointed.

Jack looked around as they climbed the stairs, his face softening as if he was remembering being a boy in this place. There must be good memories along with bittersweet ones during his four years here.

Josey felt a sudden chill along with a premonition. She tried to shake it off. Why would there be any reason to be afraid for Jack?

They were led down a long, dark hallway to an end room. "Since you're newlyweds," Enid said. "This way you won't disturb the rest of the household."

Jack arched a brow at the old woman behind her back.

"I'm sure you'll ring me on the intercom if you need anything." Enid let out an irritated snort. "Dinner is served at seven on the dot. I wouldn't be late if I were you." With that she left them standing outside the room and disappeared into the dim light of the hallway, her footfalls silent as snowfall.

"That woman is scary," Josey whispered, making Jack chuckle.

"Let's do this right," he said, surprising her as he swung her up into his arms. "In case anyone is watching," he added in a whisper.

She let out a squeal as he carried her over the threshold, making him laugh. His laughter was contagious and she found herself caught up in the moment as he kicked the door shut and carried her into the bedroom.

The room was huge, with a sitting area furnished with two chintz-covered chairs in front of a stone fireplace. Josey caught a glimpse of a large bathroom done in black-and-white tile, sheer white drapes at the open French doors to a small balcony and, at the heart of the room, a large canopied bed.

Jack slowed at the bed, and as he gently lowered her to the cool, white brocade spread his gaze met hers. The sheer white curtains billowed in, bringing with them the sweet scent of clover and pine.

She felt as if she'd been saved by a white knight and brought to the palace for safekeeping. It would have been so easy to lose herself in the deep sea-blue of his eyes as he leaned over her. Jack was incredibly handsome and charming. Everything seemed intensified after what she'd been through. The hard feel of his chest against her breasts, the slight brush of his designer stubble against her cheek, the oh-so-lusty male scent of him as he lowered her to the soft bed.

She wanted desperately to blot out everything but this. It would have been so easy, with her gaze on his sensual, full mouth, to bury her fingers in his a-little-too-long blond hair and drag him down until his lips, now just a breath away from hers, were—

"You're not thinking about kissing me, are you?" he asked, sounding as breathless as she felt. "Because that wasn't part of the bargain. Unless you want to renegotiate?"

Josey realized that he'd been about to lose himself as well, and, for whatever reason, he'd stopped himself. And her. She shouldn't be feeling safe. She should be thinking of the consequences of losing herself even for a little while in the arms of this man. Jack was making it clear what was going to happen if she opened that door.

She squeezed her hands between their bodies, pressing her palms to his muscular chest, but she didn't have to push. Jack eased slowly back to a safer distance, though it seemed to take all of his effort.

"Didn't Enid say something about dinner at seven?"

she asked, her voice sounding strange even to her ears. "I have just enough time to take a bath first."

Jack glanced toward the bathroom. He must have been wondering why she needed another bath since she'd had a shower in town.

"I can't resist that tub." A huge clawfoot tub sat in the middle of the black-and-white tiled floor.

His blue eyes darkened again with desire, and she saw both challenge and warning as he glanced from the tub to her. They were alone at this end of an empty wing pretending to be husband and wife. Unless she wanted the marriage *consummated,* she'd better be careful what signals she sent out.

Josey slid from the bed, grabbed her backpack and stepped into the bathroom, closing and locking the door behind her. The room was large. Along with the tub there was an old-fashioned sink and dressing table, and enough room to dance in front of a full-length old-fashioned mirror.

Josey set down her backpack and stepped to the tub to turn on the faucet. Enid had left her a bottle of bubble bath, bath soap and a stack of towels. As the tub filled, bubbles moved in the warm breeze that blew in from an open window in the corner and billowed the sheer white curtains.

She stripped off her clothing and, with a start, caught her reflection in the full-length mirror behind her. She looked so different. Slowly, her heart in her throat, she studied her face, then the bruises she'd been able to hide under her clothing. The raw rope burn on her neck made her wince at just the sight of it. What had she been thinking earlier with Jack? Had she lost herself in him, he would have seen—

She shuddered at the thought. She couldn't let that happen. It wouldn't be easy to keep her injuries covered so no one saw them until she had a chance to heal. But that would be easier than trying to explain them if she got caught.

Josey turned away from her unfamiliar image, anxious to climb into the tub of warm, scented water. She knew she couldn't wash away her shame any more than she could wash away the memory of what had happened.

As she stepped into the tub and slowly lowered herself into the bubbles and wonderfully warm, soothing water, she listened for Jack. Had he left the room? Or was he just on the other side of the door?

Against her will, her nipples hardened at the thought. She reminded herself that Jack was just a means to an end. A safe place to hide out until she could decide what to do. As Jack had said, the Winchester Ranch was in the middle of nowhere. Her past couldn't find her here.

Once she knew her mother was safe…

She lay back in the tub, the breeze from the window nearby stirring the bubbles, but the chill Josey felt had nothing to do with the warm spring air coming through the window.

Was she really safe here? There was something about this place, something about Jack's grandmother, definitely something about the Hoaglands, that gave her the creeps.

Josey shivered and sank deeper in the tub, realizing the most dangerous person in this house could be the man she'd be sleeping in the same room with tonight.

VIRGINIA WINCHESTER STOOD at the window where she'd watched the Cadillac convertible drive up earlier.

She hadn't been sure which nephew it was and hadn't cared. All she knew, and this she'd had to get from Enid since her mother wasn't apt to tell her, was that three nephews had confirmed that they would be arriving over the next few weeks.

She wouldn't have recognized any of them. The last time she'd seen them they'd been sniveling little boys. She'd had no more interest then than she did now.

By now there could be more. She shuddered at the thought.

She did, however, wonder why her mother hadn't just invited everyone back at the same time. Pepper had her reasons, Virginia was sure of that.

She herself was the fly in the ointment, so to speak. The letter had specified the time her mother wanted to see her. She assumed everyone else had also been given a specific time to arrive.

Virginia wasn't about to wait. She wasn't having it where her mother invited her favorites first. Virginia planned to be here to make sure she wasn't left out. So she'd come right away—to her mother's obvious irritation.

Growing up on the ranch, she'd felt as if their mother had pitted them all against each other. The only time she'd felt any kind of bond with her siblings had been their mutual jealousy, distrust and dislike of their younger brother Trace—their mother's unequivocal favorite.

Now Virginia worried that just because two of her brothers had produced offspring—at least that she knew of—the Winchester fortune would be divided to include them.

As the only daughter and oldest of Call and Pepper

Winchester's children, she deserved her fair share, and she said as much now to her mother.

Pepper sighed from her chair nearby. "You always were the generous one. Of course you would be the first to arrive and completely ignore my instructions."

"I came at once because…" Her voice trailed off as she caught herself.

"Because you thought I was dying."

The letter had clearly been a ruse to get them all back to the ranch. Virginia saw that now. Pepper Winchester didn't even look ill. "The letter from the attorney…" She floundered. There had never been anything she could say that had pleased her mother.

She'd been torn when she'd received the letter from the attorney on her mother's behalf. Her mother was dying?

The thought had come with mixed emotions. It was her *mother.* She should feel something other than contempt. Pepper had been a terrible mother: cold, unfeeling, unreachable. Virginia hadn't heard a word from her in twenty-seven years. What was she supposed to feel for her mother?

"I'm just asking that you be fair," Virginia said.

"I suppose you'd like me to cut out my grand-children?"

Like her mother had ever been a loving grandmother. "Those of us without children shouldn't be penalized for it. It's not like you would even recognize your grand-sons if you passed them on the street," Virginia pointed out.

"I also have a *granddaughter.*"

Virginia turned from the window to stare at her mother.

"McCall. Trace's daughter. She's with the sheriff's department. She's the one who solved your brother's murder and was almost killed doing so."

"McCall?" That bitch Ruby had named her kid after Virginia's father? Why wasn't Pepper having a conniption fit about this? She should have been livid. "Surely you aren't going to take the word of that tramp that this young woman is a Winchester."

Her mother's smile had a knife edge to it. "Oh, believe me, she's a Winchester. But I knew the rest of you would require more than my word on it. I have the DNA test results, if you'd like to see them."

Virginia was furious. Another person after the Winchester fortune. No, not just another person. *Trace's* daughter. Virginia felt sick.

"So I have four grandchildren I don't know," her mother corrected with sarcasm. "And there could be more, couldn't there?"

Virginia swore silently. "Why did you even bother to get the rest of us home?"

Pepper raised a brow. "I knew you'd want to see me one last time. Also I was sure you'd want to know the whole story about your brother Trace. You haven't asked."

"What is there to ask?" Virginia shot back. "His killer is dead. It was in all the papers." Trace was dead and buried. "I would think that you wouldn't want to relive any of that awfulness."

She didn't mention that Pepper had kept her other children away from Trace when he was young, as if afraid they might hurt him. Her protectiveness, along with her favoritism and love for Trace, was why they had no great love for their little brother. He'd come into their lives after they'd heard their mother couldn't have anymore children. Trace became the miracle child.

"You weren't at his memorial service," her mother said.

Virginia couldn't hold back the laugh. "Are you kidding? I didn't think I was invited." She started for the door, unable to take any more of this. "You should have warned us in the letter from your lawyer that this visit was really about Trace."

"Your brother was *murdered!* I would think something like that would give even you pause," her mother said, making Virginia stop in midstep on the way to the door.

Even her? As if she had no feelings. Her mother didn't know. Her mother knew nothing about what she'd been through. As if Pepper was the only one who'd lost a child.

"I was sorry to hear about it," Virginia said, turning again to face her mother. "I already told you that, Mother. What about your children who are still alive? The ones you *didn't* protect when they were young? Aren't we deserving of your attention for once, given what you let happen to us?"

The accusation hung in the air between them, never before spoken. Pepper's expression didn't change as she got to her feet. If Virginia hadn't seen the slight trembling in her mother's hand as she reached for her cane, she would have thought her words had fallen on deaf ears.

"You are so transparent, Virginia," her mother said, as she brushed past. "Don't worry, dear. Your trip won't be wasted."

MCCALL STOOD IN THE DUST, staring at the makeshift camp, hating the feeling this place gave her. Her deputies had gone only a few miles along the riverbank before they'd come across it and the tree where the limb had broken off and fallen into the water.

This was where they had camped. From the footprints in the mud and dirt around the area, there'd been three of them. One man, two women.

A breeze blew down the river, ruffling the dark green water. She caught the putrid odor of burned grease rising from the makeshift fire pit ringed in stones. Someone had recently cooked over the fire. A pile of crumpled, charred beer cans had been discarded in the flames and now lay charred black in the ash. Little chance of getting any prints off the cans, but still a deputy was preparing to bag them for the lab.

"We followed the tire tracks up from the river through the trees," one of the other deputies said, pointing to the way the campers had driven down the mountainside to the river. "They came in through a farmer's posted gate on a road that hadn't been used in some time."

"You think they lucked onto it or knew where they were going?" she asked. The narrow dirt road had led to this secluded spot, as if the driver of the vehicle had wanted privacy for what he had planned. If he'd just wanted to camp, he would have gone to the campground down by the bridge.

"If he knew about the road, then that would mean he could be a local," the deputy said. "I say he lucked onto the road, figuring it ended up at the river."

Like him, she didn't want to believe whoever had hung two people was from the Whitehorse area. Or worse, someone they knew. Who really knew their neighbors and what went on behind closed doors?

McCall had learned that there were people who lived hidden lives and would do anything to protect those secrets.

She watched as a deputy took photographs of the dead tree with the broken branch at the edge of the bank, watched as another made plaster casts of both the tire prints and the footprints in the camp.

"Sheriff?"

She was starting to hate hearing that word. She turned to see the deputy with the camera pointing into the river just feet off the bank.

"I think we found the missing car."

Chapter Four

Jack listened to the soft lap of water, fighting the image of his "wife" neck deep in that big old tub just beyond the bathroom door.

This definitely could have been a mistake. He felt a surge of warring emotions. A very male part of him wanted to protect her and had from the moment he'd stopped to pick her up on the highway.

But an equally male part of him was stirred by a growing desire for her. Josey was sexy as hell. To make matters worse, there was a vulnerability in her beautiful green eyes that suckered him in.

His taking a "wife" had been both brilliant and dangerous. The truth was he didn't have any idea who this woman in the next room was. All he knew was that she was running from something. Why else agree to pretend to be his wife for a week? The thought worried him a little as he glanced toward the bathroom door.

The sweet scent of lilac drifted out from behind the closed and locked door. But nothing could shut out the thought of her. After having her in his arms, it wasn't that hard to picture her lush, lanky body in the steamy bathroom: the full breasts, the slim waist and hips, the long, sensual legs.

The provocative image was almost his undoing. He groaned and headed for the door. He couldn't let her distract him from his real reason for coming back to Montana and the Winchester Ranch—and that was impossible with her just feet away covered in bubbles.

Opening their bedroom door, he headed down the hallway toward the opposite wing—the wing where he and his mother had lived twenty-seven years ago.

Jack had expected to find his mother's room changed. As he opened the door, he saw that it looked exactly as he remembered. The only new addition was the dust. His boots left prints as he crossed the floor and opened the window, needing to let some air into the room.

The fresh air helped. He stood breathing it in, thinking of his mother. She'd been a small, blond woman who'd mistakenly fallen in love with a Winchester. She'd been happy here—and miserable. He hadn't understood why until later, when he'd found out that Angus Winchester was his father.

His jaw tightened as he considered the part his grandmother had played in destroying Angus Winchester, and that reminded him of the reception she'd given him earlier when he and Josey had arrived.

He shouldn't have been surprised. When he was a boy, Pepper hadn't paid him any mind, as if he were invisible. They'd all lived in some part of the huge old lodge, but seldom crossed paths except at meals.

It wasn't that she'd disliked him. She just hadn't cared one way or the other, and finding out he was Angus's child hadn't changed that.

He stood for a moment in the room, promising his mother's memory that he'd see that Pepper Winchester paid for all of it, every miserable day she'd spent in this house or on Earth. Then he closed the window and left the room, anxious to get back to Josey.

Who knew what a woman on the run with a trail of secrets shadowing her might do.

FROM THE TUB, Josey glanced over at her backpack resting on the floor of the bathroom. Just the sight of it turned her stomach, but she was pretty sure she'd heard Jack leave and she had no idea how long he might be gone.

She quickly climbed from the tub and didn't bother to towel off. Instead, she grabbed the robe he'd bought her and avoided looking in the mirror at her battered body. She also avoided thinking about how she'd gotten herself into such a mess. She was sick to death of all the "if only" thoughts.

As the saying went, the die was cast.

All she knew was that she couldn't keep carrying her backpack around like a second skin. She'd seen the way Jack had eyed it. He was more than a little curious about what was so important in it that she wouldn't let it out of her sight, and he'd eventually have a look.

Which meant she had to find a safe place for its contents.

She listened. No sound outside the bathroom door. Hefting the backpack, she cautiously opened the door a crack. The room appeared to be empty.

She shoved the door open a little wider, not trusting that he hadn't returned.

No Jack. She wondered where he'd gone. She wondered a lot of things about him, but mostly why he'd wanted her to masquerade as his wife. He'd have to have seen she was in bad shape when he'd picked her up on the highway.

So what was in it for him? After meeting his grand-mother, Josey was pretty sure it couldn't be money. She just hadn't figured out what Jack was really after.

Josey reminded herself it had nothing to do with her. All she had to do was play her part, hide out here on this isolated ranch until the heat died down. No one could find her here, right?

She quickly surveyed the room. She couldn't chance a hiding place outside this room for fear someone would find it.

Across the room, she spotted the old armoire. The wardrobe was deep, and when she opened it she saw that it was filled with old clothing.

Strange. Just like this huge master suite. Who had it belonged to? she wondered, as she dug out a space at the back, then opened her backpack.

The gun lay on top. She grimaced at the sight of it. Picking it up, she stuck the weapon in the robe pocket. What lay beneath it was even more distressing. The money was in crisp new bills, bundled in stacks of hundreds. Over a million dollars splattered with blood.

Hurriedly she dumped the bundles of cash into the back of the wardrobe, hating that she had to touch it. Blood money, she thought. But the only way to save her mother. And ultimately, maybe herself.

She quickly covered it with some old clothing. Then, grabbing some of the clothing still on hangers, she stuffed the clothes into the backpack until it looked as it had.

Straightening, she closed the wardrobe and looked

around to make sure Jack wouldn't notice anything amiss when he returned.

Footsteps in the hallway. She started. Jack? Or someone else?

As she rushed back into the bathroom, closed and locked the door, she stood for a moment trying to catch her breath and not cry. Seeing the gun and the bloody money had brought it all back.

She heard the bedroom door open and close.

"You all right in there?" Jack asked. Her heart pounded at how close a call that had been.

Discarding the robe, she quickly stepped back into the tub. "Fine," she called back, hating that she sounded breathless.

"We're going to be late for supper if you don't move it."

The water was now lukewarm, the bubbles gone. She slid down into it anyway and picked up the soap. Her hands felt dirty after touching the money. Her whole body did. She scrubbed her hands, thinking of Lady Macbeth. *Out, damned spots.*

Suddenly she remembered the gun she'd stuffed into the robe pocket. She rinsed, stepped from the tub and pulled the plug. The water began to drain noisily as she looked around for a good place to hide the weapon.

There were few options. Opening a cabinet next to the sink, she shoved the gun behind a stack of towels on the bottom shelf. It would have to do for now until she could find a better place to hide it.

She intended to keep the weapon where she could get to it—just in case she needed it. That, unfortunately, was a real possibility.

WHEN JOSEY CAME OUT of the bathroom, she wore another of the Western shirts he'd bought her in town and the new pair of jeans that fit her curves to perfection. Jack had also picked her out a pair of Western boots, knowing she would need them to horseback-ride during their week on the ranch.

Jack grinned, pleased with himself but wondering why she hadn't worn the two sexy sundresses he'd picked out for her. He'd been looking forward to seeing her in one of them, and he said as much.

"Maybe I'm a jeans and boots kind of girl," she said.

She looked more like a corporate kind of girl who wore business suits and high heels, he thought, and wondered where that had come from. "You look damned fine in whatever you wear."

She appeared embarrassed, which surprised him. The woman was beautiful. She must have had her share of compliments from men before.

As he smiled at her, he couldn't help wondering who she was—just as he had from the moment he'd spotted her on the highway with her thumb out. Josey carried herself in a way that said she wasn't just smart and savvy, she was confident in who she was. This woman was the kind who would be missed.

Someone would be looking for her. If they weren't already.

Jack warned himself not to get involved, then laughed to himself at how foolish that was. He could have just dropped her off beside the road. Or taken her as far as the town of Whitehorse, given her some money and washed his hands of her and her troubles. He should have.

But something about her...

Jack shook his head. He'd played hero and sold himself on the idea of a wife for this visit with his grandmother, and now he worried he'd bought himself more than he could handle as he looked at her.

Her face was flushed from her bath, the scent of lilac wafting through the large bedroom. The Western shirt she'd chosen was a pale green check that was perfect for her coloring and went well with the scarf that she'd tied around her neck. The two scarves had been her idea.

She looked sweet enough to eat and smelled heavenly. It was going to be hell being around her 24/7 without wanting more than a pretend marriage.

Worse, their charade required a modicum of intimacy with her. As he led her down to dinner, he put his hand against the flat of her back and felt the heat of her skin through the thin cotton of her shirt. The touch burned him like a brand.

She looked over at him. Her smile said she knew what he was up to. He smiled back. She had no idea.

"Finally," said a woman impatiently from the parlor where they'd been shown in earlier.

Jack looked in to see his aunt Virginia, a glass of wine in her hand and a frown on her less than comely face. The years hadn't been kind to her. The alcohol she'd apparently already consumed added to her overall disheveled look.

Her lipstick was smeared, her linen dress was wrinkled from where she'd been perched on the arm of one of the leather chairs and there was a run in her stockings.

"We eat at seven sharp," she snapped, and pointed to the clock on the wall, which read several minutes after.

Josey started to apologize, since it was her fault for staying in the tub so long, but the other woman in the room cut her off.

"You remember Virginia," Pepper Winchester said drily.

"Of course, Virginia," Jack said, extending his hand.

His aunt gave him the weakest of handshakes. "Mother says you're Angus's son?" Like his grandmother, Virginia had also missed her brother's funeral. *Nothing like a close-knit family,* Jack thought.

Virginia was studying him as if under a microscope. Her sour expression said she saw no Winchester resemblance. "The nanny's child." She crinkled her nose in distaste. "Dear Angus," she said, as if that explained it.

Jack tried not to take offense, but it was hard given the reception he and his pretend wife were getting here. He reminded himself that this wasn't a social visit. Once he got what he'd come for, he would never see any of them again.

"This is my wife, Josey," he said, glad as hell he hadn't come here alone. All his misgivings earlier about bringing her were forgotten as he slipped his arm around her slim waist and pulled her close.

JOSEY FELT JACK'S ARM tighten around her as Virginia gave her a barely perceptible handshake.

It was hard not to see the resemblance between mother and daughter, Josey thought. Both women were tall, dark-haired and wore their bitterness on their faces. Virginia was broader, more matronly and perhaps more embittered as she narrowed her gaze at Josey, measuring her for a moment before dismissing her entirely.

"Can we please eat now?" Virginia demanded. "I'm famished. Little more than crumbs were served for lunch. I hope dinner will prove more filling." She turned on her heel and headed down the hall.

Josey turned to Pepper, who was reaching for her cane. "I do apologize. I'm afraid I enjoyed your wonderful tub longer than I'd meant to. That is such a beautiful bathroom. I especially like the black-and-white tiles."

Pepper seemed startled. "Enid put you in the room at the end of the south wing?" She quickly waved the question away. "Of course she would. Never mind."

Grabbing her cane, she followed her daughter down the hallway. Josey noted that Pepper Winchester was more feeble than she let on. Maybe she really was dying. Or maybe just upset.

"I knew it," Josey whispered to Jack, as they followed Pepper at a distance toward the dining room. "That room must have been your grandmother's and grandfather's. Wouldn't Enid know that putting us in there would upset your grandmother?"

"I would bet on it," he said.

Josey followed his gaze to where Enid stood in the kitchen doorway, looking like the cat who ate the canary. "She must have shared that room with your grandfather. I wonder why she moved out of it?"

Jack chuckled and slowed, lowering his voice as they neared the dining room. "I doubt it was for sentimental reasons. My mother told me that according to Winchester lore, Pepper didn't shed a tear when my grandfather rode off and was never seen again. She just went on running the ranch as if Call Winchester had never existed—until her youngest son Trace vanished."

DINNER WAS A TORTUROUS AFFAIR. Jack had known it wouldn't be easy returning to the ranch, but he hadn't anticipated the wellspring of emotions it brought to the surface. As he sat at the dining room table, he half expected to see his mother through the open kitchen doorway.

It was at that scarred kitchen table that he and his mother had eaten with the Winchester grandchildren and the staff. In the old days, he'd been told, Pepper and Call had eaten alone in the dining room while their young children had eaten in the kitchen.

But Call had been gone when his mother came to work here, and Pepper had eaten with her then-grown children in the dining room. When Trace was home, his mother had heard Pepper laughing. After Trace eloped with that woman in town and moved in with her, the laughter stopped. Jack's mother said she often didn't hear a peep out of the dining room the entire meal with Pepper and her other children.

"The animosity was so thick in the air you could choke on it," his mother had told him. "Mrs. Winchester took to having her meals in her room."

"Well, Mother, when are you planning to tell us what is really going on?" Virginia demanded now, slicing through the tense silence that had fallen around the table. She sat on her mother's right, Jack and Josey across from her. Her face was flushed; she'd clearly drunk too much wine. Most of dinner she'd complained under her breath about Enid's cooking.

Jack had hardly tasted his meal. He'd pushed his food

around his plate, lost in the past. Josey had seemed to have no such problem. She'd eaten as if she hadn't had a meal for sometime. He wondered how long it had been.

Pepper had also seemed starved, cleaning her plate with a gusto that didn't go unnoticed. For a dying woman, she had a healthy appetite. Almost everyone commented on it, including Enid when she'd cleared away the dishes before bringing in dessert.

"Well, Mother?" Virginia repeated her demand.

Enid had stopped in midmotion and looked at Pepper, as if as anxious as any of them to hear why the family had been invited back to the ranch.

"Isn't it possible that I wanted my family around me after receiving such horrible news about your brother?" Pepper asked, motioning for Enid to put down the cake and leave the room.

Virginia scoffed at the idea. "After twenty-seven years you suddenly remembered that you had other family?"

"Does it matter what brought us together?" Jack spoke up. "We're here now. I assume some of the others will be arriving, as well?" he asked his grandmother.

She gave him a small smile. "A few have responded to my invitation. I knew it would be too much to have everyone here at the same time, so the others will be coming later."

"Well, I know for a fact that my brother Brand isn't coming," Virginia said unkindly. "He's made it perfectly clear he couldn't care less about you or your money." She poured herself the last of the red wine, splashing some onto the white tablecloth. "In fact, he said he wouldn't come back here even if someone held a gun to his head."

"How nice of you to point that out," Pepper said.

Enid had left, but returned with a serving knife, and saw the mess Virginia had made. She set the knife beside the cake and began to complain under her breath about how overworked she already was without having to remove wine stains from the linens.

"That will be enough," Pepper said to the cook-housekeeper. "Please close the kitchen door on your way out."

Enid gave her a dirty look, but left the room, slamming the door behind her. But Jack saw through the gap under the door that Enid had stopped just on the other side and was now hovering there, listening.

"I only mention Brand to point out that not everyone is so forgiving as I am," Virginia said. She glanced at her mother, tears welling in her eyes. "You hurt us all, Mother. Some of us are trying our best to forgive and forget."

"Let's not get maudlin. You're too old, Virginia, to keep blaming me for the way your life turned out."

"Am I? Who do *you* blame, Mother?"

A gasp came from behind the kitchen door.

Pepper ignored both the gasp and her daughter's question as she began to dish up the cake. "I've always been fond of lemon. What about you, Josey?" she asked, as she passed her a slice.

Josey seemed surprised at the sudden turn in conversation. "I like lemon."

Pepper graced her with a rare smile that actually reached the older woman's eyes. "I don't believe you told me how you and my grandson met."

"I was hitchhiking and he picked me up," Josey said.

Jack laughed, as he saw Josey flush at her own honesty. "It was love at first sight." He shot her a look that could have melted the icing on her cake.

Her flush deepened.

"She climbed into my car and, as they say, the rest is history," Jack said.

Pepper was studying Josey with an intensity that worried him. The elderly woman seemed to see more than he had originally given her credit for. Did his grandmother suspect the marriage was a ruse?

"Well, how fortunate," Pepper said, shifting her gaze to Jack. "You're a lucky man." Her smile for him had a little more bite in it. "You have definitely proven that you're a Winchester."

Jack chuckled, afraid that was no compliment. It didn't matter. He could tell that his grandmother liked Josey and he would use that to his advantage. But it wouldn't change the way he felt about his grandmother.

He'd spent most of dinner secretly studying his beautiful "wife." Josey continued to surprise him. Her manners and the way she carried herself made him realize she must have come from money—probably attended a boarding school, then some Ivy League college. She seemed to fit in here in a way that made her seem more like a Winchester than he ever could. So how did she end up on the side of the road with nothing more than a backpack? And more importantly, why would a woman with her obvious pedigree be sitting here now, pretending to be his wife?

"You've hardly touched your food."

Jack dragged his gaze away from Josey as he realized

his grandmother was talking to *him.* "I guess I'm not really hungry."

Pepper nodded. "You probably have other things on your mind."

"Yes. I should apologize for making this trip into a honeymoon. It wasn't my intention when I answered your letter."

"No, I'm sure it wasn't," his grandmother said with a wry smile. "But what better place than the family ranch? I assume you remember growing up here. You loved to ride horses. Surely you'll want to ride while you're here and show Josey the ranch. You were old enough to remember your uncle Trace, weren't you?"

Virginia didn't bother to stifle a groan.

Her mother ignored her. "You must have been—"

"Six," Jack said, and felt all eyes at the table on him. Beside him, he sensed that even Josey had tensed.

"Then you remember the birthday party I threw for him?"

Jack nodded slowly. It wasn't likely he would forget that day. His mother told him years later that Pepper had been making plans for weeks. Everything had to be perfect.

"I think she really thought that if she threw him an amazing birthday party, Trace would come back to the ranch," his mother had told him. "Of course the only way he was welcome back was without the woman he'd eloped with, the woman who was carrying his child. Or at least he thought was carrying his child. Pepper didn't believe it for a moment. Or didn't want to."

"I had a cake flown in," Pepper said, her eyes bright with memory. "I wanted it to be a birthday he would never forget." Her voice trailed off, now thick with emotion.

Instead it had been a birthday that none of the rest of them had ever forgotten. His grandmother, hysterical with grief and disappointment when Trace hadn't shown for the party, had thrown everyone off the ranch, except for Enid and Alfred Hoagland.

"I bought all the children little party hats," she was saying. "Do you remember?"

From the moment he'd received the letter from his grandmother's attorney, Jack had known she wanted something from him. He just hadn't been sure what. But he had an inkling he was about to find out.

"I recall sending all of you upstairs so you wouldn't be underfoot," Pepper said. "I believe you were playing with my other grandchildren at the time." Her gaze locked with his, and he felt an icy chill climb up his spine and settle around his neck. "Whose idea was it to go up to the room on the third floor? The one you were all forbidden to enter?"

THIS FAR NORTH it was still light out, but it would be getting dark soon. Deputy Sheriff McCall Winchester listened to the whine of the tow truck cable, her focus on the dark green water of the Missouri River.

Déjà vu. Just last month, she'd watched another vehicle being pulled from deep water. Like now she'd feared they'd find a body inside it.

A car bumper broke the surface. The moment the windshield came into view, McCall felt a wave of relief not to see a face behind the glass. Which didn't mean there still wasn't someone in the car, but she was hoping that bizarre as this case was so far, it wouldn't get any worse.

The tow truck pulled the newer-model luxury car from the water to the riverbank, then shut off the cable motor and truck engine. Silence swept in. Fortunately they were far enough upriver on a stretch of private ranch land away from the highway, so they hadn't attracted any attention.

McCall stepped over to the car as water continued to run out from the cracks around the doors. She peered in, again thankful to find the car empty of bodies. Snapping on latex gloves, she opened the driver side door and let the rest of the water rush out.

Along with river water, there were numerous fast food containers, pop cans, empty potato chip bags.

"Looks like they were living in the car," a deputy said.

McCall noticed something lodged under the brake pedal.

"Get me an evidence bag," she ordered, and reached in to pull out a brand-new, expensive-looking loafer size 10½.

"The driver got out but left behind his shoe?" a deputy said as he opened the passenger-side door. "But did he make it out of the water?"

"See if you can find any tracks downstream," McCall said. "The current is strong enough here that he would have been washed downriver a ways."

"Should be easy to track him since he is wearing only one shoe," the deputy said.

"Let's try to find out before it gets dark," McCall said. Otherwise they would be dragging the river come morning for a third body.

On the other side of the car, a deputy pulled on a pair of latex gloves and opened the passenger-side door to get into the glove box. McCall watched him carefully check the soaking wet registration.

"The car is registered to a Ray Allan Evans Jr., age thirty-five, of Palm City, California. Looks like he just purchased the car three days ago."

Chapter Five

Josey felt the air in the dining room tremble with expectation as she waited for Jack to answer his grandmother. What was this about a room that he'd been forbidden to enter?

"What would make you think I've been in that room?" Jack said, meeting his grandmother's gaze with his cold blue one.

His grandmother's look was sharp as an ice pick. She knew, just as Josey sensed, that he was evading the question. But why would he care about something that happened when he was six?

And why would his grandmother care after all these years?

"Those cute little party hats you were all wearing when you went upstairs," his grandmother said. "I found them in the room."

"Really?" Jack said, forking the piece of the cake Pepper had passed him. "I'm afraid I don't remember anything about some party hats."

"Is that right?" His grandmother's tone called him a liar. "Are you going to also tell me you don't remember that day?"

"Oh, I remember that day. I remember my mother

losing her job and us having to leave the ranch, the only home I'd ever known," Jack said in a voice Josey barely recognized. "I remember my mother being terrified that she wouldn't be able to support us since Angus had been cut off without a cent and didn't have the skills or the desire to find a job. I remember looking at the Winchester Ranch in the rearview mirror and you standing there, making sure we all left and didn't come back."

"Oh, my," Virginia said, clearly enjoying Jack's rancor at her mother.

"I remember Angus losing himself in the bottle and my mother struggling to take care of us while she tried to make us a family," Jack said, his voice flat and cold. "I remember the toll it took on her. But nothing like the toll being exiled from here took on Angus."

"Your mother. Is she…?" Virginia asked.

"She died a year before Angus drank himself to death."

Pepper looked down at her untouched cake. "I didn't know."

"Really? Then you didn't know he left a note?" Jack reached into his pocket and took out a piece of folded, yellowed paper. Josey saw that it was splattered with something dark and felt her stomach roil.

Jack tossed the note to his grandmother. "It's made out to you." With that he got to his feet, throwing down his cloth napkin. "If you'll excuse me."

McCALL SAT in her patrol car, studying the screen. The moment she'd typed in Ray Allan Evans Jr.'s name, it had come up. Ray Jr. was a person of interest in a homicide in Palm City, California. The murder victim was his father, Ray Allan Evans Sr. He'd been killed two days ago—just a day after his son had purchased a very expensive luxury automobile.

She put through a call to the detective in charge of the case in the Palm City homicide department, Detective Carlos Diaz. She told him that she'd found Ray Jr.'s car and that he was wanted in Montana for questioning in another homicide case.

She asked what they had on the Evans murder so far.

"A neighbor can place Ray Jr. at the house at the time of the murder. But he wasn't alone. His stepsister was also there. Her car was found on the property. No staff on the premises, apparently, which in itself is unusual. This place is a mansion with a full staff, at least a couple of them live-in."

"I'm sorry, did you say his *stepsister?*" McCall asked, thinking of the young Jane Doe the fisherman had hooked into.

"Josephine Vanderliner, twenty-eight, daughter of Harry Vanderliner, the founder of Vanderliner Oil. The father is deceased. The mother married Evans two years ago, was in a car accident shortly afterward, suffered brain damage and is now in a nursing home. The step-daughter had been in a legal battle over money with Evans Sr. Her fingerprints were found on the murder weapon. Neither Vanderliner or Evans Jr. has been seen since the night of the murder."

"What's the story on Ray Jr.?"

"Goes by RJ. Thirty-four, no visible means of support, lives with his father."

And yet he'd purchased himself a new expensive car on the day his father was murdered?

"The housekeeper found Ray Sr.'s body—and the

safe—wide-open. She says she saw Ray Sr. putting a large amount of cash into the safe just that morning. According to the eyewitness, RJ and his stepsister left together in a large, newer-model black car at around the time of death estimated by the coroner. Didn't get a make and model on the car."

"Sounds like the one we just pulled from the Missouri River."

McCall filled him in on what they had so far— one female victim in the same age range as Josephine Vanderliner and a car registered to Ray Allan Evans Jr., driver missing and suspected drowned. "We're dragging the river now for a possible third body," she told him.

Detective Diaz sent her photographs of both Ray Jr. and Vanderliner.

McCall watched them come up on her screen. Ray Evans Jr. first. A good-looking, obviously rich kid from the sneer on his face. She thought of the abuse her Jane Doe had suffered before being hanged and drowned. Did he look like a man capable of that? Or was he also a victim of foul play?

McCall held her breath as she clicked on the photograph of Josephine Vanderliner.

JOSEY TOUCHED HER NAPKIN to the corner of her mouth, then carefully placed it beside her dessert dish before rising to follow her "husband" outside.

"That was awkward," she heard Aunt Virginia say, as Josey left the dining room. "So what does the note say?"

"Not now, Virginia."

"He killed himself because of you, didn't he?"

As Josey reached the front door she heard what

sounded like a slap followed by a cry and glass breaking. She didn't look back as she pushed open the door
and stepped out into the fresh air.

Spotting Jack down by the barn, she walked in that
direction, just glad to be out of the house. She figured
Jack wanted to be alone and certainly wouldn't want her
company. For appearance's sake, she had needed to go
after her husband. She hadn't wanted to feel his pain,
but her own emotional pain was so near the surface and
had been for too long. She knew family drama and how
it could tear you apart from the inside out.

Josey slowed as she neared. He stood with his back
to her, his head high as if he were gazing out across the
ranch. The sun hung over the Little Rockies in the far
distance, the sky ran from horizon to horizon, so wide
and deep blue, she could understand why Montana was
called Big Sky Country.

Jack didn't look at her as she joined him at the corral
fence. He'd opened himself up back there at dinner, and
even though she hadn't known him long, she was sure he
regretted it. He'd exposed how vulnerable he'd been, still
was, when it came to his grandmother and the past.

Against her will, Josey felt a kinship with him. Life
hadn't been kind to him, and yet she sensed a strength
in him born of hard times. Jack might have taken a beat-
ing, but he wasn't down for the count, she would bet on
that.

"Did you enjoy my sad tale?" he asked, still without
looking at her.

She sensed the last thing he needed right now was
her sympathy. "It was a real heartbreaker. Was any of
it true?"

He looked over at her and grinned. "It almost brought a tear to the old bat's eye, don't you think?"

"I could tell it broke your aunt Virginia's heart."

He laughed and slipped his arm around her, his gaze going back to the sunset. "I can't believe how lucky I was to find you."

She might have argued that, but she was smart enough to keep those thoughts to herself. As long as no one discovered where she'd gone, they were both lucky.

"Have you ever seen anything more beautiful?" he asked, looking toward the horizon.

"No." She studied the wild landscape, broken only by a few outcroppings of rock and the dark tops of the cottonwoods. Between the ranch and horizon was a deep ravine that seemed to cut the place off from the world.

"The Winchester Ranch is the largest ranch in three counties," Jack said.

"So it's the money you're after?"

He smiled. "Who says I'm after anything?" He pulled her closer as he turned them back toward the ranch lodge.

Josey had seen how upset he'd been at dinner. Maybe he wasn't after his grandmother's money, which was just as well because Josey doubted he would be getting any. But he was after something, and that something felt more like settling a score with his grandmother.

She felt a chill as they walked arm in arm back to the lodge, wondering what his grandmother was after and why she was bringing the family back to the ranch.

Whatever Jack was up to, his grandmother had her own agenda, Josey thought. Out of the corner of her eye she saw a face at one of the lodge windows.

Pepper Winchester's face appeared for an instant before the curtain fell back into place.

THE PHOTOGRAPH OF VANDERLINER was several years old, but there was no mistake. She wasn't the Jane Doe now lying in the county morgue.

So who was the victim they'd pulled from the river?

"Our Jane Doe isn't Vanderliner," McCall told Detective Diaz. She promised to get back to him as soon as they were able to run the dead woman's prints.

Back down at the river, the surface golden with the last of the sun's rays, McCall listened to the sound of the boat motor as her fiancé, Game Warden Luke Crawford, helped drag the river for the bodies.

Because of the lack of manpower in a county sheriff's department, game wardens were often called in, since they had the same training as other law enforcement in the state.

Normally crime in and around Whitehorse was mostly calls involving barking dogs, noisy neighbors or drunk and disorderlies. Occasionally there would be a domestic dispute or a call to check on an elderly person who wasn't answering her phone.

Murder was rare, but not unheard of. McCall knew that firsthand. She'd had more than her share of bloodshed recently. The last thing she wanted was another homicide.

"So if the driver of the vehicle was able to swim to safety, he's on foot," George said.

McCall nodded, glancing down river toward Highway 191.

"You're thinking someone picked him up," George

said with a nod. He sounded exhausted. "Makes sense. He would probably need medical attention. I'll call the hospital emergency rooms." He headed for his vehicle.

"You don't have to stick around. I can call you if we find another body."

He shook his head. "I want to be here."

"Thanks." McCall turned back to the river. If RJ wasn't in the river, he'd be on the hunt for shoes, dry clothing, a vehicle and possibly medical attention, as George had said.

So what would he do? Head for the highway. The nearest town was Whitehorse to the north, but she doubted he'd be picky if he could catch a ride. If he was headed south he'd probably have to go clear to Billings to get what he needed. Or cut over to Lewistown, which was closer.

George came back to tell her that a man matching RJ's description or a woman matching Josephine Vanderliner's hadn't come into emergency rooms in Whitehorse or Lewistown.

"So either he wasn't hurt that badly or he hasn't gotten to a place where he can get medical attention," McCall said, glancing behind her into the tall pines. Vanderliner, she could only assume, was in the river.

She heard one of the search-and-rescue volunteers call her name. "Got something down here," the volunteer called.

McCall worked her way down the river to where the volunteer stood next to something caught in a limb beside the water. She shone her flashlight on the object. A leather shoulder bag.

Squatting down and pulling on her latex gloves,

she dragged the bag to her and opened it. A wallet. She focused her flashlight beam on the driver's license inside—and the photograph of a pretty, ginger-haired young woman. The name was Josephine Vanderliner.

PEPPER STEPPED BACK from the window, trembling inside with rage and embarrassment. How dare they condemn her? Couldn't they understand how devastated she'd been to lose Trace?

She brushed angrily at her tears. She wasn't looking for their sympathy. Nor their understanding. And it was a damned good thing, because clearly she would get neither.

She felt the note she'd stuffed into her pocket and eased it out. The paper was yellowed. The dark splatters made her recoil. Angus's suicide note. She didn't have to open it to know that he was blaming her even from the grave.

What about the failings of his father? Where was their anger toward the man who had gone to such extremes, spoiling them rotten one moment and then punishing them by locking them in that third-floor room?

She thought of the young wife she'd been. The foolish young woman who'd let Call Winchester rule all their lives for way too long.

Funny, she was still acutely disappointed in him even after all these years. Her anger had eased as did her fear of him, she thought with no small amount of irony, but not her disappointment.

Was it any wonder that she had never trusted another man? Even Hunt McCormick. How different her life would have been if she'd run off with him like he'd wanted her to.

She shook her head at the very thought. She hadn't been able to leave because of her children, children she should have protected from Call. All her children, not just Trace. But the older ones had always been Call's children from the time they were born, and she'd felt so helpless against him back then.

The truth was she'd loved Call, trusted him to do what was best for all of them, even when it came to how their children should be raised.

She'd been blinded by that love.

Until Trace was born.

Pepper would never know what had changed. Maybe she'd finally seen Call for what he was, a bully. Or maybe she'd finally fallen out of love with him.

Either way, she'd been determined to save Trace from him. That struggle had definitely killed any love she had for her husband and had cost her the rest of her children.

Pepper knew that some people thought she was cold and heartless. They pointed to her reaction when Call hadn't come back from his horseback ride more than forty years ago. She hadn't been able to hide her relief that he was gone.

But her secret shame was that a part of her still loved the Call she thought she'd married. Just as a part of her still loved Hunt McCormick.

She started to unfold the note, bracing herself, but changed her mind and dropped the paper into the wastebasket. For a long moment she stood there, staring down at Angus's last cry for help. The one thing she'd never been was a coward. At seventy-two, she couldn't start now. She bent down to retrieve the note and carefully eased the paper open.

The words were scrawled and almost illegible. The handwriting of a child. Or a terrified, sick man.

I'm so sorry, Mother. Forgive me. I forgive you. Angus.

She crumpled the note in her fist, suddenly unable to catch her breath or stem the flow of tears. Her body jerked with the shuddering sobs that rose up in her. It was all she could do not to scream out her anguish.

Pepper didn't hear the door open behind her.

"I thought you might need something," Enid said, making her spin around in surprise. Enid held a teacup and saucer.

Pepper could smell the strong tea, strong to cover up the drugs her housekeeper had been systematically and surreptitiously giving her for years. At first Pepper hadn't noticed, she'd been so grateful for the oblivion. She assumed it made Enid's job easier having Pepper either out like a light or so docile she wasn't any trouble.

But after learning about Trace, things had to change. She needed her wits about her. She also needed to be more careful when it came to Enid.

She quickly turned her back to Enid, stepping to the window to hastily dry her tears and pull herself together. Enid was the last person she wanted seeing her like this.

She heard the elderly housekeeper set down the cup and saucer on the end table by the bed and move to join her at the window. Enid pulled back the curtain wider to see what Pepper had been looking at out the window.

She smiled smugly as she saw what Pepper did—Jack and Josey walking arm in arm toward the house.

"I brought you up some chamomile tea to help you sleep." Enid motioned toward the cup she'd put down beside Pepper's bed.

"You are so thoughtful," Pepper said, not bothering to hide the sarcasm in her tone.

"Yes, aren't I," Enid said and turned to leave. "Good night."

"Good night," Pepper repeated, just wanting the woman to leave her room.

"Drink your tea while it's hot."

She bristled. "Please close the door behind you." Pepper didn't turn until she heard the door close.

The smell of the strong tea made her nauseous as she stepped to the door and locked it, then she picked up the cup of tea and carried it into the bathroom, where she paused before pouring it down the drain.

Tonight she could have used the mind-numbing effect of whatever drug Enid had put in it. But she could no longer allow herself that escape.

She dumped the tea and rinsed out the sink. The cup she left by her bed before going to the window to look out across the deep ravine to the rocky point in the distance.

It was over there, just across from the ranch, that her precious son had been murdered. Pepper thought of the third-floor room, the binoculars she'd found, and the feeling lodged deep in her heart that someone in her own family was involved.

Nothing else mattered but finding out the truth. It was why she'd made sure her granddaughter McCall had become acting sheriff. While they had never discussed it, Pepper had seen something in McCall's expression.

She didn't believe, any more than Pepper did, that the alleged, now-deceased killer had acted alone.

And McCall, who was so like her grandmother, would never let a killer go free. Pepper was counting on her.

AS THEY ENTERED THE HOUSE, Jack discovered his aunt Virginia had been waiting for them.

"I'd like to speak to my nephew," she said, looking pointedly at Josey. *"Alone."*

"Anything you have to say, you can say in front of my wife," he said indignantly.

"It's okay," Josey said, touching his arm. "I'd like to take a look around the ranch."

"Don't go far," Jack said.

Josey looked amused.

"I'm just saying this is wild country and you can get turned around out there in the dark."

"Yes," Virginia agreed with a tight smile. "My father disappeared out there on a night a lot like this one."

"I don't want you disappearing, too," Jack said, only half-joking. "Also, there are rattlesnakes out there."

Josey glanced at his aunt as if to say, *And in here, too.*

"What is this about?" Jack asked his aunt, as Josey left.

"Why don't we step down the hall?" she said. "That awful woman might be listening. Both awful women," she added under her breath.

They stepped into the parlor. Virginia closed the door and spun around, clearly angry. "Okay, you can knock off the act."

"I beg your pardon?"

"You aren't Angus's son, and even if you are, you're not getting this ranch."

Jack had to smile. "Isn't it possible I'm just here to see my grandmother?"

His aunt scoffed. "You don't have to pretend with me. She can barely stand the sight of you. She isn't going to leave you a thing."

Jack was tempted to say that it seemed to him that Pepper Winchester couldn't stand the sight of anyone, maybe especially her daughter. "Frankly, I think she'll try to take it all with her before she leaves any of us a dime. But even if I'm wrong, I'm no threat to you."

Virginia looked skeptical. "*Please.* After that sympathy play you made at dinner? I see what you're doing, but it won't work. You're wasting your time."

"Is that why you pulled me in here? To tell me that?"

Virginia was tall like her mother, but without the grace. "Has my mother mentioned who else is coming to this gruesome reunion?"

"Your mother hasn't shared anything with me."

"Well, I'm worried." Her gaze bored into his. "I heard Enid and Alfred whispering between themselves. They seem to think Pepper might not be of sound mind. I'm betting they're thinking that they can somehow have her put away and take all her money."

Jack wasn't surprised to hear this. "God knows they've put up with her long enough. They probably deserve it." Enid acted as if she was the lady of the house, not Pepper. It surprised him that his obstinate grandmother put up with it.

"What Enid and Alfred Hoagland deserve is to be fired before they steal her blind," Virginia snapped.

"What if they've somehow coerced her into making a new will and leaving everything to them?"

"I can't see Pepper doing that under any circumstances. Haven't you seen the way she looks at Enid? She detests the woman. And no one is going to have Pepper committed. It would require a mental evaluation, and I'd put my money on Pepper passing with flying colors."

"You'd put *your* money on it?" Virginia said. "As if you had any money. I know that's not your car parked out there." She gave him a satisfied look. "I have connections. I had the plates run. That Cadillac belongs to the Galaxy Corporation. I assume you're employed by them. Or did you steal the car?"

"I borrowed the Caddie with every intention of taking it back," Jack said, bristling. He hadn't expected this of his aunt.

"And your *wife?* Did you borrow her, as well?" Virginia asked with a laugh, then waved it off. "I was only joking. She's right up your alley. I've seen the way she looks around the lodge, as if she's putting a price tag on all the furnishings."

Jack bit back an angry retort. It was one thing to come after him, but it was another to go after his wife. Even his pretend wife.

The irony didn't escape him. He was defending a woman he'd picked up on the highway. A stranger he didn't know beans about. But then, neither did his aunt.

"Josey likes antiques and comes from money," he said, feeling that might be true. "I can assure you, she isn't interested in Grandmother's."

"You don't look anything like Angus," Virginia said, changing tactics.

Jack laughed, determined not to let his aunt get to him. "I'm not going to argue this with you. My grandmother knows the truth, that's all that matters."

"Your *grandmother* is the reason you're a bastard. She didn't think your mother was good enough for Angus."

He tried to rein in his temper, but Virginia had pushed him too far. "Pepper never approved of any of the women her sons fell in love with. Or her daughter, for that matter. She controlled you all with money and a cushy life on this ranch. All except Trace. Is that why you hated him so much—because he couldn't be bought?"

The color had washed from Virginia's face. She stood trembling all over, her lips moving, but nothing coming out.

"But the truth is I wasn't the only bastard to come out of this house—was I, Aunt Virginia?"

JOSEY WALKED UP the narrow dirt road to a small hill before she stopped to look back at the sprawling lodge and the tall cottonwoods and the sparse pines that made the place look like an oasis in the desert.

The lodge was far enough off the main road that she felt relatively safe. From what she'd seen earlier, the main road got little use, not that the lodge could be seen by anyone just happening to drive past.

No one knew she was here. That was the beauty of it. So why couldn't she relax? Because her mother wouldn't be safe until she sent the money and got her moved.

Jack had said they would stay for the week, but Josey knew she couldn't make it that long. If there was just some way to send the money without having to leave here—or let anyone know where she was, she thought, as she walked back down the road in the diminishing daylight. It would be dark soon, and she had no desire to be caught out here alone.

But she wouldn't involve Jack any more than she had. She couldn't.

As she entered, she didn't hear a sound from down the hall. The door to the parlor was closed. She assumed Jack was still in there talking to his aunt, though she couldn't imagine what they might have to talk about. Unless Virginia was trying to talk him into doing away with Pepper and splitting the take.

They'd better cut Enid and Alfred in, Josey thought with a wry smile. The two gave her the creeps. If anyone was plotting to knock off Pepper it was one or both of them.

As she opened the door to the bedroom, Josey realized that Jack could have finished his talk with his aunt and be waiting here for her.

She was relieved to see the bedroom unoccupied. She closed the door behind her and stood looking at the large canopied bed. Playing married was one thing. But where was Jack planning to sleep?

The door opened behind her as if on cue. She turned to look at him, and he grinned as if he knew exactly what she'd been thinking.

"I'm sorry, where did you say you would be sleeping?" she asked.

"I was thinking we could negotiate something."

She smiled back at him. "Think again."

"I suppose sharing the bed is out of the question?"

"You suppose right."

"Don't you trust me?"

"Not as far as I can throw you."

"Now, honey," he said, reaching for her, "we can't let Enid catch us sleeping separately on our honeymoon."

Josey stepped away from him. "We can if we have a fight." She picked up a cheap vase from a nearby table, tossing it from hand to hand. "A lover's quarrel. You know newlyweds."

He was shaking his head, but still smiling. "No one will hear it if you break that."

"But Enid will see the broken glass in the morning when she comes with the coffee and catches you sleeping in that chair over there."

Jack launched himself at her and the vase, but he wasn't fast enough. The vase hit the floor and shattered like a gunshot. Jack's momentum drove them both back. They crashed into the bed and onto it, with Jack ending up on top.

"Now this is more like it," he said, grinning down at her.

Josey could feel the hard beat of his heart against her chest as she looked into those amazing blue eyes of his. The man really was adorable.

"I want to kiss you," he said quietly. He touched her cheek, his fingers warm.

She felt a small tremor. He could be so gentle that it made her ache.

"What will it cost me?"

"You want to pay for a kiss?" she asked, raising a brow, trying to hide her disappointment that he hadn't just kissed her.

"Is there any other way you'd let me kiss you?"

She hated that he made her sound cheap and mercenary. She'd only agreed to take his money for this week because it would have made him suspicious if she'd turned it down. Did he really think she was doing this for the money?

"I really—" The rest of her words caught in her throat as she realized he was untying her scarf. She grabbed for the ends to stop him—just not quickly enough.

"What the hell?" He pushed off her to a sitting position on the edge of the bed next to her, his expression one of shock and horror as he stared at her. "Josey... what—"

"It's nothing." She quickly sat up as she tried to retie the scarf to cover up the rope burn on her neck.

"Like hell," he said, reaching out to stop her as he took in the extent of her injury. "How did this happen?"

She didn't answer as she tried to take the ends of the scarf from him and retie them. "Please."

He held the scarf for a moment longer, his expression softening as he lifted his gaze to hers. "Who did this to you?" There was an edge to his voice, a fury.

"It has nothing to do with you." She pulled away, getting to her feet and turning her back to him as she clumsily tied the scarf with trembling fingers.

"This is why you were on the highway," he said, rising from the bed to come up behind her. "This is what you're running from."

She didn't deny it.

"I don't understand why—"

"No, you don't, so just forget it," she snapped. She finished tying the scarf and swung around to face him. "I took care of it."

He stared at her. "The only way to take care of it is to kill the person who did this to you."

Josey didn't dare speak into the dense silence that fell between them.

Jack seemed to be waiting for her to explain. When she didn't, he let out a curse.

She watched him grab one of the pillows and a quilt that had been folded up on the end of the bed. He brushed past her and dropped both the pillow and quilt onto the chair before leaving the room.

It was much later that she heard him return to the dark room and curl up in the chair across from her. She could hear him breathing softly and feel his gaze on her. She closed her eyes tight and told herself she didn't give a damn what Jack Winchester thought of her. It wasn't the first night she'd gone to sleep lying to herself.

She woke up just after two in the morning to find Jack gone.

Chapter Six

It was late by the time McCall reached her office in Whitehorse. She had brought evidence from the crime scene that needed to be sent to the lab in Missoula first thing in the morning.

Deputies had discovered a bullet on the outside of the car pulled from the river and in the headrest on the driver's side. Both were .38 slugs. Someone in camp had been armed. Deputies would continue their search in the morning for the weapon—and any more victims.

But McCall wasn't ruling out that at least one person had gotten away—possibly armed—from the crime scene.

"Any chance you'll be coming down to my place later?" Luke had asked as he rubbed the tension from her shoulders before she'd left the crime scene.

McCall had leaned into his strong hands, wanting nothing more than to spend the night with Luke in his small trailer curled against him. He was staying in the trailer out on his property until he completed their house. He planned to have it done before their Christmas wedding so they could move in together.

She couldn't believe how lucky she was that Luke had come back into her life.

"I'm sorry," she'd told him. "I'd better stay at my place near town tonight. This case—"

"I know." He'd turned her to smile at her, then kissed her.

He did know. He knew how much this job meant to her even though she'd fought taking the acting sheriff position. He'd encouraged her to run for sheriff when the time came.

"You sound like my grandmother," she'd said.

"Yeah? Well, we both know you aren't finished with your father's death, don't we?"

It was the first time he'd mentioned what he'd overheard the night he'd saved her life at her cabin. She hadn't had to answer, since there was no point. He was right. She wasn't finished, and she had a bad feeling her grandmother wasn't, either.

McCall pushed aside thoughts of her fiancé as she went to work.

George had assisted with taking their Jane Doe's prints. McCall entered them now into the system and waited. The chance of getting a match was slim at best. The Jane Doe would have had to been arrested, served in the military or had a job where her prints were required for security reasons.

That was why McCall was amazed when she got a match.

Her prints had come up from a prostitution charge. She'd served eight months and had only recently been released. Her name was Celeste Leigh of Palm City, California. No known address or place of employment. She was twenty-two and believed to be living on the streets.

McCall put in a call to Detective Diaz in Palm City

and wasn't surprised to find him still at work. Apparently he was getting a lot of pressure on the Ray Allan Evans Sr. murder because Evans had been the husband of Ella Vanderliner.

"I've got an ID on our Jane Doe," she said and proceeded to tell him about Celeste Leigh.

"Prostitution? I'm not surprised. From what we've discovered investigating his father's homicide, RJ was involved in a string of shady ventures that lost money, and his daddy had to bail him out. He was also known to frequent the lower end of town."

"Celeste was wearing a diamond engagement ring with a big rock on it. We found the receipt for it in the glove box of the car. It set RJ back a large chunk of change. Which might explain why her ring finger appeared to have been broken. I think RJ changed his mind about any upcoming nuptials."

Diaz swore. "The bastard broke her finger trying to take back the wedding ring? I guess I shouldn't be surprised given that he later hung her from a tree."

"Apparently, he'd been abusing her for some time."

"That fits with what we know about him. He'd been accused by other prostitutes of abuse, but they always dropped the charges. So what about the other noose?"

"We found Josephine Vanderliner's purse downriver from where RJ and Celeste were believed to have been camped. We'll continue dragging the river in the morning. Given the three sets of tracks, the two nooses and her purse, we're fairly certain Vanderliner was there with them."

"Keep me updated. I'll see if I can find some next of kin that need to be notified of Celeste Leigh's death."

McCall hung up and studied the photograph of Ray

Allan Evans Jr. again. He was blond, blue-eyed, movie-star handsome, but there was something about him that unnerved her, and would have even if she hadn't known anything about him.

It was in the eyes, she thought, as she pushed away the photograph and looked instead at the copy she'd made of Josephine Vanderliner's photo.

Vanderliner was pretty in a startling way. In the photo, she had her long, ginger-colored hair pulled back and wound in a loose braid. Her eyes were aquamarine, and she was smiling into the camera as if she didn't have a care in the world.

That had apparently changed, McCall thought, as she sighed and made another copy of the photographs to take to the *Milk River Courier* office come morning.

If there was even a chance that either RJ Evans or Josephine Vanderliner were still in the area, then residents needed to know and be on the lookout for them.

If they were in Whitehorse, the town was small enough that any stranger stood out like a sore thumb— especially this time of year. During summer a few tourists would past through on what was known as the Hi-Line, Highway 2 across the top part of Montana. But it was a little early for tourist season.

As McCall locked up and headed for her cabin beside Milk River, she glanced at the vehicles parked diagonally at the curb in front of the bars. None from out of state. Only one from out of town.

She left the mostly sleeping little Western town and headed home, praying neither suspect was anywhere near Whitehorse, Montana.

WHERE WAS JACK? Josey felt a chill as she glanced around the empty room. The door to the bathroom was open, the room empty.

She sat up, listening. The house seemed unusually quiet. Eerily so. She had a sudden urge to get out of there while she had a chance. What was wrong with her?

From the open window next to the bed, she heard one of the horses whinny, then another. She threw her legs over the side of the bed and hurried to the window.

A wedge of moon and a zillion tiny stars lit the black night. She could make out the horses moving around the corral as if something had set them off. She waited for her eyes to adjust to the darkness, surprised that the floodlight near the barn was out.

It had been casting a golden glow over the ranch yard earlier when she'd gone to bed. Her pulse quickened.

A breeze rustled the leaves of the cottonwoods, casting eerie shadows in the direction of the lodge.

Among the shadows, something moved.

Jack.

He crept along the dark edge of the buildings like a man who didn't want to be seen. He had something in his hand that occasionally caught the moonlight. A crowbar?

Josey watched him reach the end of the far wing, the one she'd noticed was older than the rest and had boards over the windows and doors. He disappeared around the corner.

Where was he sneaking off to at this time of the night and why? Apparently, she wasn't the only one with secrets.

JOSEY WOKE THE NEXT MORNING to the sound of running water. A few minutes later Jack came out of the bathroom wearing only his jeans and boots. His muscled chest was suntanned and glistening. He smelled of soap, his face was clean shaven, his blond hair was wet and dark against the nape of his neck.

She'd felt a wave of desire wash over her.

"Morning," he said, seeing she was awake. He seemed to avoid her gaze.

"Good morning." Well, if he wasn't going to say anything, then she was. "Jack—"

"I'll let you get ready and come down with you for breakfast," he said quickly. "Can you be ready in half an hour?"

She nodded, sensing the change in him. She'd hoped things would go back to the way they were yesterday, when he'd been playful and affectionate. It had been a game, this pretend marriage. But apparently yesterday had changed that after he'd seen the rope burn on her neck. Or did it have something to do with his late-night exploration?

She'd heard him come in just before daylight. He hadn't turned on a light. She'd listened to him stumbling around in the dark and caught a whiff of alcohol. Had he been drinking?

Now he didn't give her a second glance as he pulled on a Western shirt and left.

She lay in bed, hating this change in him. She knew he must be regretting picking her up on the highway, let alone proposing marriage, even a fake one. She touched the rope burn on her neck. What he must think of her.

If he only knew.

Well, what did he expect? she thought angrily, as she swung her legs over the side of the bed and headed for the bathroom. He didn't know a thing about her. He hadn't wanted to know a thing about her. All he wanted was a pretend wife to fool his grandmother. And she'd done her job just fine.

She took a quick bath and was ready when he returned.

He again gave her only a glance, his gaze pausing for a moment on the new scarf she had tied around her neck. She couldn't wait for her neck to heal enough that she could dispense with the scarves.

As they descended the stairs, Josey missed his warm hand on her back. She missed his touch almost as much as she missed the way he had looked at her.

Jack's grandmother glanced up as they entered the dining room, her gaze narrowing. The old gal didn't miss much. She must see that there was trouble in honeymoon paradise.

Josey felt uncomfortable, as if she was under scrutiny throughout breakfast. Even Virginia seemed to pick up on the fact that something was different between Josey and Jack.

"The two of you should take a horseback ride," Pepper Winchester said as they finished breakfast. "Show her the ranch, Jack. I know how you love to ride."

Josey started to say that wasn't necessary, that she didn't know how to ride, that the last thing the two of them needed was to be alone together, but Jack interrupted her before she could.

"I think that's a great idea," he said, getting to his feet. "I'll go saddle up two horses and meet you in the barn."

JACK WAS ALMOST SURPRISED when he turned to find Josey framed in the barn doorway. He wondered how long she'd been standing there watching him. A while, from her expression.

He hated the way he'd been treating her since seeing what some bastard had done to her. He couldn't help his anger. He wanted to kill the son of a bitch.

A part of him also wanted to grab Josey and shake some sense into her. How could she have let something like this happen? Clearly, she'd gotten hooked up with the wrong guy. Why had he thought her too smart to fall for a man like that? He was disappointed in her.

But it only amplified the fact that he didn't know this woman. Apparently not at all.

"You've never ridden a horse before, have you?" he said now. "I saw your expression at breakfast."

"That had more to do with you than horses," she said, as she stepped into the barn. "I woke up last night and you were gone."

He finished cinching down the saddle and turned to her. "I went downstairs for a drink."

Her eyes narrowed. "Before or after you sneaked outside with a crowbar?" she asked. She started to turn away when he grabbed her arm and swung her back around to face him.

"What are you doing here with me?" he demanded.

She looked into his eyes, and he lost himself for a moment in that sea of green. "I didn't have anything better to do."

He let go of her arm, shaking his head. "So we're both lying to each other. Be honest with me and I'll be honest with you," he challenged. "What are you running from? Or should I say *who* are you running from?"

She took a step back. "Whatever you're doing here, it's none of my business."

He laughed. "Just like whoever is after you is none of my business?"

"It's better if you don't know."

He gave her an impatient look. "I'd like to know what has you so scared."

"No, you don't." With that she turned as if to leave, but collided with Alfred Hoagland, who was standing just outside.

"I came to see if you needed help saddling the horses," the old man said, his two large hands on each of her shoulders to steady her. "Change your mind about going for a ride?"

"No," she said, pulling free of him and stepping back into the barn.

"I've got it covered, Alfred," Jack said.

The old man stood in the doorway for a moment. "Fine with me," he said before turning away.

Jack stepped past Josey to make sure Alfred wasn't still standing outside listening.

"Do you think he heard what we were saying?" she whispered behind him.

"Don't worry about it." He turned his back to her.

"Look, if you've changed your mind about this marriage—"

"I haven't," he quickly interrupted. "I'm sorry about the way I've been acting. Coming back here..." He waved a hand through the air. "It's hard to explain. I have a lot of conflicting emotions going on right now. But I'm glad you're here with me. Come for a ride with me. It's a beautiful day, and Enid packed us a lunch so we can be gone until suppertime. You have to admit, that has its appeal."

IT DID. Just like Jack did when he smiled the way he was smiling at her now. Earlier, she'd stood quietly studying him from the barn doorway as he saddled the horses. He'd been unaware she was there and she hadn't said anything, enjoying watching him.

He'd spoken softly to each horse, touching and stroking the horses in such a gentle way that she'd found herself enthralled by this side of the man.

Now she eyed her horse, wondering what she'd gotten herself into. Her horse, like Jack's, was huge. She told herself she could handle this. After everything she'd been through, this should be easy.

But when she looked at Jack she didn't feel strong or tough. She felt scared and hurt. It was crazy that what he thought of her could hurt so much, and it scared her that she cared. She barely knew this man she was pretending to be wed to, and his sneaking away from their room last night proved it.

Worse, she couldn't help thinking about what his reaction would be if he knew the truth. She cringed at the thought.

"Ready?" Jack swung up into his saddle with a fluid, graceful motion that made her jealous. Everything seemed to come easy for him, making her wonder about the story he'd told at dinner last night.

Apparently, he'd had a hard life, and yet it didn't show on him. Unless his bruises were deeper than her own.

She concentrated on attempting to copy Jack's movements. She grabbed hold of the saddle horn and tried to pull herself up enough to get a foot in the stirrup.

She heard Jack chuckle and climb down from his horse.

"Here, let me help you." He didn't sound upset with

her anymore. She wished that didn't make her as happy
as it did. "Put your foot in my hands."

She looked into his face, overcome by the gentleness
she saw there, and felt tears well in her eyes. She hurriedly put her booted foot into his clasped hands and,
balancing herself with one hand on his shoulder, was
lifted up and into the saddle.

The horse shuddered, and she grabbed the saddle
horn with both hands, feeling way too high above the
ground.

"Thank you," she said, furtively wiping at her
tears.

"You don't have to do this."

He misread the reason for her tears. She nodded, not
looking at him. What was wrong with her? She hadn't
shed a tear throughout her recent ordeal, and here she
was fighting tears? She was letting Jack Winchester get
to her. Big mistake.

"I want to do this." She could feel his gaze on her
and was relieved when he walked around and climbed
back on his horse.

As her horse followed Jack's out of the barn, she
looked at the vast country and took a deep breath. Her
father always told her she could do anything she set her
mind to. But her father had been gone for years now,
and her mother no longer knew her.

They rode through tall green grass across rolling
prairie, the air smelling sweet with clover. In the distance, Josey could see the dark outline of a mountain
range. Jack told her they were the Little Rockies.

They'd ridden from rocky dry land covered with
nothing but cactus and sagebrush into this lush, pine-
studded, beautiful country. It surprised her how quickly

the landscape changed. Even the colors. They ran in shades of silken green to deep purple by the time they reached the horizon.

They stopped on a high ridge deep in the Missouri Breaks. She felt as if she was on top of the world, the land running wide-open to the horizons as clouds bobbed in a sea of blue overhead. "It's amazing up here," she said, taking an awed breath.

"It's still lonely country," he said. "There isn't anything for miles."

"Your grandmother doesn't run cattle or grow any crops?"

"She used to, back when the family all lived on the ranch, but I'm sure she sold off the herd after we all left," Jack said. "All she had was Enid and Alfred, and you can tell by the shape the place is in that they haven't been able to keep up with maintaining the house and barns. I'm surprised she kept the horses, but I suspect Alfred must ride. I wouldn't imagine my grandmother's been on a horse in years."

"You used to ride as a boy?" she guessed.

He nodded. "My mother and I rode down here. It was our favorite spot."

She heard a wistfulness in his voice that she hadn't heard since they'd been here, a love for this country and a sorrow for the mother he'd loved.

"You miss this," she said.

He chuckled.

She could almost feel the battle going on inside him. He'd come here to even a score with his grandmother in some way. But a part of him wanted this, not the money, but the land, and not just to own it, but to ranch it.

"What would you do if your grandmother asked you to stay?"

"She won't."

"How can you be so sure of that?"

"Because I know her."

"Maybe she's changed."

He chuckled again. "Right. Anyway, it's too late."

Was it ever too late? She thought of RJ. Maybe some people were too bitter, too sick, too hateful to ever change. Maybe Jack's grandmother was one of them.

She listened to the breeze blow through the boughs of the ponderosa pines and wished she and Jack never had to go back to civilization.

"I'd run cattle on it the way this ranch was when I was a kid," Jack said suddenly. "I'd get wheat growing up on those high benches and alfalfa and hay. I'd make it a working ranch again instead of..." His voice trailed off and he laughed, as if at his own foolishness. "Just talking," he said. "I came up here to say goodbye."

They ate the lunch Enid had packed them with a view of the lake where the Missouri River widened into Fort Peck Reservoir. The water looked like a sparkling blue jewel hidden in this untamed, uninhabited country.

"I'm sorry about the way I reacted last night," Jack said after they'd finished a sandwich and soda on a large flat rock.

She nodded, a lump in her throat. This was the last thing she wanted to talk about.

"I was just so angry at the person who did that to you..." His voice trailed off. "And I took that anger out on you."

She understood more than he knew.

"Josey, I want to help."

She shook her head. "You don't know any more about me than I do you. I think it is best if we leave it that way."

"That's not true. You've met my family. You know where I was born. Hell, you practically know my whole life history."

"Just up to the age of six. I don't even know where you live now."

"Wyoming. Ten Sleep, Wyoming. How about you?"

She shook her head.

"Look, I know you're in trouble and it's because of a dangerous man." He raised his hand to keep her from interrupting him. Not that she was going to. So far he'd been dead-on. "All I'm saying is that maybe I can help."

Josey smiled, her eyes burning with tears again. She was touched and hated that she was. "Don't be so nice to me, okay?"

"I can't help myself." His gaze locked with hers.

She felt the heat in those eyes, the blue like a hot flame. Their thighs brushed as he moved, the touch sending a flurry of emotions racing through her.

Jack drew her into his arms before she could protest. His mouth dropped to hers as his strong arms encircled her.

His kiss was filled with passion and heat and, strangely enough, a gentleness like he'd shown with the horses, as if he knew to go easy with her because she would spook easily.

She did more than let him kiss her. She kissed him back, matching his passion and his heat, if not his gentleness, until she came to her senses and drew back.

He was looking at her, his eyes filled with a soft tenderness.

It was as if a dam burst. All the tears she'd repressed for so long broke free. He pulled her back into his arms, holding her as she sobbed, his large hand rubbing her back as he whispered soothing words she could neither hear nor understand.

McCALL STOOD OUTSIDE the cold, sterile autopsy room waiting for George to come out and give her the results. The crime lab had flown in personnel to do the autopsy. George was assisting.

She'd had only a few hours' sleep before she'd called down to the Missouri River this morning to check with Luke. They were dragging the river and had been since daylight. So far, nothing.

George didn't look so hot as he came out of the autopsy room. "I figured you'd be waiting." He made her sound ghoulish. "The report should be typed up within an hour."

She shook her head. She didn't want to wait that long. "Just give me the highlights."

He sighed, looking exhausted and a little green around the gills. She figured he regretted taking this job and wondered how long he'd last.

"Could we at least sit down for minute?" he asked, and headed for the conference room.

She grabbed them both a cup of coffee from the machine and joined him.

"As you know, she had numerous signs of abuse," he said, as she handed him a cup of coffee and sat down. "Scars, cuts and bruises, cigarette burns. She had either been with a long-time abuser or..."

"She got off on it," McCall guessed.

He grimaced.

"So maybe the hanging was a sexual thing."

George looked even more uncomfortable. "With two women? There were two places where ropes had been tied to the limb."

McCall thought about it for a few moments as she sipped her coffee. "Maybe we were wrong about there being another victim. Maybe he'd hung her up there before and the limb had held the first time. This time, it didn't."

"I guess. But how do you explain the car in the river?"

She shook her head. "I guess it would depend on whether or not they were alone at that camp. We've just assumed Vanderliner was with the other two because she was seen with her stepbrother leaving the scene of the murder and we found her purse."

McCall rubbed her temples. "Also there were at least three different sets of footprints found at the scene, two women's-size types of sneakers and tracks that matched the loafer we found stuck under the brake pedal of the car."

"You're thinking the victim on the slab could have had more than one pair of sneakers," George offered.

"Or the other prints could be those of the missing Josephine Vanderliner. It would explain the other noose, and we have three different hair samples from the car, which was only a couple of days old. We know Vanderliner was in the car at some point because of the eye-witness but we don't know for how long. He could have dumped her and kept her purse."

"So we don't know if Vanderliner made it as far as Montana."

McCall nodded thoughtfully. "I just have a bad feeling she's here. Either in that river or on the loose. I stopped by the newspaper office early this morning. They're running photographs of both RJ Evans and Josephine Vanderliner. If either of them got out of that river, then someone has to have seen them. They were going to need a ride since the only tracks we found were for the car in the river."

"Great," George said. "One of them abuses women for the fun of it and the other is wanted for murder." He shook his head. "I hope you put something in the paper to warn residents in case they come across them."

"Armed and dangerous and possibly traveling together."

Chapter Seven

RJ felt like hell. His shoulder had quit bleeding. Fortunately the bullet had only furrowed through his flesh and missed the bone, but it hurt like a son of a bitch. He knew he had to get some antibiotics. If it wasn't already infected.

But right now he was more concerned about the blow to his head. The double vision was driving him crazy. That and the killer headache. Bitches.

Celeste had almost drowned him. Josey had shot him. He'd been damned lucky to get out of that car. He wondered where Celeste was. The last he'd seen her she had been sucked out of the car by the current.

He'd gotten his foot caught under the brake pedal. When he'd finally freed himself, he'd come up downriver in time to see Josey getting away. He'd been bleeding like a stuck pig and was half-blind from the blow on his head, but even crazed as he was, he knew he had to catch her or everything he'd worked for would turn to a pile of crap.

How had things gone so wrong? Maybe Celeste was right. Maybe it had been when he'd lost his temper and strung her up from that tree limb. He hadn't meant to kill her, just shut her the hell up.

No, where things had really gone haywire was when he decided to string up Josey next to her. Should have known that limb couldn't hold both of them. Shouldn't have left the pistol lying on that log by the fire pit, either.

But who knew either of those women could move that fast? He hadn't been that surprised when Josey had shot him. He'd expected something like that from her, but he'd never seen it coming with Celeste. She'd been like a wild animal when she'd attacked him.

He'd tied the ropes to the bumper of the car and strung up both women. When the damned limb broke, he'd thrown the car in Reverse, thinking he could run them down. But then Josey had shot at him and Celeste had come flying in the driver-side window at him, the rope still around her neck and dragging in the dirt. She'd knocked the breath out of him.

And with her pummeling him he hadn't realized he was still in Reverse, the car still going backward toward the river. The next thing he knew the car was in the river and he was underwater and Celeste, that stupid whore, was still fighting him.

Shuddering now at the memory of how close he'd come to drowning, he stumbled and almost fell. He'd climbed out of the river and gone after Josey. He knew she'd make a run for it. No surprise, she'd taken the backpack with the money and his gun in it.

He'd climbed the hill back to the single-track dirt road. That was when he'd spotted her. She had shoes, so she had made better time than him. He'd lost both of his in the river, and he was shot and hurt, and with nothing but socks on his bare feet the ground felt rough.

He'd seen her on the highway halfway up the

mountainside. Too far away to shoot her even if he'd had the pistol. Maybe with a rifle...

But then a pale yellow Cadillac convertible had roared across the bridge and up the other side, stopping three-quarters of the way up the mountain when the driver saw Josey standing beside the road.

RJ had picked up a rock and thrown it as hard as he could. It hit on the mountain below him and rolled down, starting a small avalanche. But of course it hadn't stopped Josey from disappearing in the Cadillac.

He didn't know how far he walked last night. He just knew he had to put some distance between him and the river. He'd finally laid down under a big pine tree and slept until daylight. The soles of his feet were bleeding through his socks.

He'd awakened this morning and realized he could see the highway from where he was on the side of the mountain and the cop cars. All that commotion. They must have found Celeste.

That was when he knew he was in trouble. He had to find Josey before the cops did. But he couldn't track her down in the shape he was in. He needed shoes, clothes, a vehicle, medicine and some drugs. He'd lost his stash in the car when it went into the water. He felt jittery and irritable. Soon his skin would be crawling as if there were bugs just under the surface.

He knew he couldn't get a ride. Not as bad as he looked. Not with cops and searchers crawling the area.

That's when he'd seen what appeared to be a roof in the distance and remembered when he and his father had come to Montana for an elk hunt. There used to be a bar at what was called Mobridge. As he remembered, there was also a house. Was it possible someone still lived there?

JACK LEANED BACK, the rock warm, the view incredible, and studied Josey.

She stood on the edge of the ravine, staring out at the wild terrain.

They hadn't spoken since the kiss or her tears. He'd held her until she'd quit crying, then she'd stepped out of his arms, seeming embarrassed, and walked to the edge of the ridge.

He'd waited, giving her time and space. He knew better than to try to push her and yet he wanted desperately to know who had done those things to her and what had her running so scared. What the hell kind of trouble had she gotten herself into and how could he make it right?

Jack chuckled to himself, realizing he'd been wanting to make things right since he was a boy and he'd seen the pain his mother had suffered.

With Josey, it was more complicated. She didn't want to involve him. Didn't she realize he was already involved? He'd become involved the moment he'd picked her up on the highway. He'd only gotten in deeper by kissing her. He wanted to help her. And if that meant getting this bastard who'd done this to her...

She'd said she'd taken care of it. He didn't like the sound of that. Had she killed the man? Was that why she was so afraid? Why hadn't she gone to the police then? Between the rope burn around her neck and the bruises he'd only glimpsed, she would have had a good case for self-defense.

The breeze ruffled her short, dark curls. He watched her raise her hand to push it out of her eyes. She was so beautiful. So strong and yet so fragile.

He knew he shouldn't have kissed her. But he hadn't been able to help himself. And he couldn't even promise that he wouldn't do it again.

She turned to look back at him. "I'm sorry about that."

"I'm not. I'm used to women crying after I kiss them." Just as he'd hoped, she smiled. "I suppose we'd better head back. We have a long ride ahead of us. Can't have Aunt Virginia passing out from hunger if we're late for supper. She is such a delicate thing."

Josey chuckled. "She's a lot like your grandmother that way."

"Isn't she though." He handed Josey her reins and helped her into her saddle.

"I'm from California, an only child, my father is dead, my mother—" Her voice broke. "She was in a car accident and never fully recovered."

"I'm sorry."

"I probably shouldn't have even told you that," she said, looking toward the horizon. "The less you know about me, the better off you'll be once I'm gone."

WITH JACK AND JOSEY OFF on a horseback ride and Virginia napping, Pepper Winchester took advantage of being alone with Enid.

She'd managed to keep her housekeeper from drugging her for some time now by getting rid of the food or drink Enid gave her privately, but she had to put a stop to it. Pepper knew her only hesitation was that she didn't want to have to fire Enid and her husband.

Not because she felt any kind of loyalty to them. She'd been more than generous with the two over the years. They must have a nice little nest egg put away.

No, it was because she didn't like change. The last thing she wanted was strangers on the ranch. Enid and Alfred had been fixtures on the place since Pepper herself had come to the ranch as a new bride. Was it any wonder they felt they belonged here even more than she did?

But she couldn't let Enid run roughshod over her anymore. Nor could she trust the woman. Pepper was sure the two wondered what she was up to. They knew her well enough to know that getting her family back to the ranch hadn't been an act of sentiment.

She found Enid in the kitchen stirring something boiling on the stove. It was impossible to tell what she was cooking. The woman really was a horrible cook. When Call was alive and the kids were all on the ranch, they'd had a real cook and Enid had been the housekeeper.

Once everyone was gone, there had been no reason to keep on anyone else, although Pepper couldn't remember firing the rest of the staff.

She suspected Enid had done it, since Pepper had been so distraught that her housekeeper and caretaker had taken advantage of it.

"Please turn that off," she said now to Enid.

Enid turned slowly to stare at her as if she couldn't believe what she was seeing. Had it been that long since she'd been in this kitchen?

Enid turned off the burner, then crossed her arms over her chest, leaning back against the counter next to the stove. "Well?"

Pepper bristled at Enid's insolent manner. She'd let

this happen and had only herself to blame. In her grief, she'd given up control of her home and her life to this woman and her husband. She now saw what a mistake that had been.

"I'm going to have to let you and your husband go." Her words seemed to hang in the humid kitchen air, surprising them both.

She waited for Enid to put up an argument. When she didn't, Pepper added, "I'm sorry."

To her surprise, Enid began to laugh. "Alfred and I aren't going anywhere."

Pepper couldn't believe her ears. "I beg your pardon?"

"You best give it some thought," Enid said, and started to turn back to whatever she was cooking.

Pepper felt her temper rise. "I've made up my mind."

Enid sighed and turned back to her, eyes narrowing into menacing slits. "Do you know how long I've been on this ranch?"

"That doesn't have anything to—"

"I've been here since before Call brought you here. I've heard every argument, seen it all, *know* you better than you know yourself." She lowered her voice. "*I* know where all the bodies are buried."

"Are you threatening to blackmail me?" Pepper demanded, barely able to contain her rage.

"If I wanted to blackmail you I could have done it a long time ago." Enid smiled. "Even now I wonder what that new acting sheriff would think if I told her just half of what I know about her grandmother."

Pepper's stomach twisted into a knot at the mention of McCall. Her heart was pounding so hard in her ears she had to steady herself, her hand going to the kitchen counter for support.

"I'd hate to see you have to spend the rest of your golden years behind bars." Enid sounded so self-satisfied that Pepper had to restrain herself from picking up one of the kitchen knives and ending this right here.

She might have done just that, except then she couldn't finish what she'd started. But once she knew the truth about Trace's murder...

"So, to answer your question," Enid was saying, "of course I'm not blackmailing you. I'm just saying you might want to reconsider." Enid turned and picked up the spoon she'd laid down earlier. "Of course, if you saw fit to put a little something in your will for Alfred and me, that would be greatly appreciated. We *have* been loyal servants on the Winchester Ranch almost our whole lives. Call, bless his soul, always said he didn't know what he would have done without us."

Pepper's gaze bored into the woman's back like a bullet at the mention of Call's name. She felt powerless and hated the feeling, even knowing that it wouldn't be for long. The day would come when she would turn the tables on Enid and it would be soon if she had anything to do with it.

"Why don't you sit down and have some of this soup I made?" Enid said. "You can tell me what you're up to getting your family back here to the ranch." She glanced over her shoulder at Pepper. "I told you, I know you better than you know yourself."

If that were true, Pepper thought, then Enid would be terrified of her and what she had planned for her.

"You're mistaken about my motives," Pepper managed to say, and started to leave the room. "I just wanted to see my family."

She was almost to the door when Enid's words stopped her.

"Some people think you've already lost your mind, locking yourself up all these years in this old place," Enid was saying. "Wouldn't take much for someone to think you're not in your right mind. Now why don't you sit down and have a little soup. I made it special just for you. It will calm you right down."

Pepper turned back to watch Enid ladle out a cup of the soup and stir something into it before setting the cup on the kitchen table.

"You'll want to eat it while it's still hot."

She stared at the cup of watery-looking soup, Enid's threat still ringing in her ears as she stepped back into the room, sat down at the table and picked up her spoon.

"A little of my soup, that's all you need," Enid said, as she went back to work at the stove.

Pepper took a bite. She gagged a little, the bile rising in her throat. She took another bite and felt the warmth of the soup and the drugs take hold. She put down her spoon.

Enid took the rest of the cup of soup and dumped it down the drain. "You should lie down for a while. You look a little peaked. I'm sure you'll feel better after a nap."

DINNER WAS A SOLEMN AFFAIR. Josey noticed that Jack's grandmother was especially quiet. Virginia drank her wine without incident, and Jack seemed lost in his own thoughts.

She was grateful he hadn't wanted to talk about what had happened on their ride. Josey was embarrassed. She never cried like that, especially in front of a stranger. And she needed to remember that was exactly what Jack was—a stranger.

As soon as dinner was over, she excused herself, saying she needed a little air, and went outside for a walk.

The air felt close. She was taken with the wild openness of this place. She could literally see for miles.

Josey thought about her mother and felt that old pain and frustration. For months she'd been trying to help her. Now she'd made things worse.

But once she got money wired to the new health-care facility and knew for sure that her mother had been moved...

She hadn't realized how far she'd gone until she turned around to head back. The sky had darkened. Thunderheads hunkered on the horizon to the west, and the wind had picked up, sending dust swirling around her. She raised her hand to shield her eyes, squinting in the direction of the Winchester Ranch lodge.

Lights were on downstairs. Fortunately, as Josey was leaving the house, Pepper had grabbed Jack, insisting he come with her. Otherwise, Josey was sure Jack would have wanted to tag along. She knew he worried about her and, like her, he must worry that the trouble after her might somehow find her here.

As she neared the house, the first drops of rain began to fall. The Cadillac sat out front where they'd left it yesterday, the top down. She noticed the keys were in the ignition, opened the driver-side door and slid behind the wheel. She whirred the top up, snapping it into place, then put up the windows and sat for a moment in the warm quiet, listening to the rain patter on the canvas roof.

She looked toward the house and thought of Jack. Through the parlor window, she could see shadows moving around inside. Jack and his grandmother?

Feeling almost guilty, she reached over and opened the glove box and dug around inside until she found the car registration.

The car was registered to Galaxy Corporation. The address was a post office box in Ten Sleep, Wyoming.

What was the Galaxy Corporation? And did this car even belong to Jack Winchester?

Josey hurriedly put the registration back in the glove box along with the Montana map, then changed her mind and opened the map.

Just as she had suspected. The town of Whitehorse had been circled. She struggled to read what had been written off to the east of it. Winchester Ranch.

A sliver of worry burrowed under Josey's skin as she stuffed everything back into the glove box and closed it.

She sat in the car, listening to the patter of the rain, staring at the old Western ranch lodge and wondering who she was pretending to be married to.

JACK HADN'T WANTED to let Josey out of his sight, but he'd been cornered by his grandmother after dinner and had no choice.

A fire burned in the small rock fireplace. It crackled softly as Pepper Winchester motioned for him to sit opposite her in the matching leather chairs.

"I'm sorry I ambushed you the other day," she said. "I shouldn't have done that."

Pepper Winchester apologizing?

"I had hoped you might have remembered something from the day of Trace's birthday party."

What was it she wanted him to remember? he wondered. Or was it something she wanted to make sure he didn't remember?

Suddenly, the room felt cold as a chill ran the length of his spine.

"I foolishly thought that if I just asked you right out, you would tell me the truth," she was saying.

Jack smiled to himself. Now this was more like his grandmother. He said nothing, waiting for the barrage he knew would follow. What he wasn't ready for was the tears as his grandmother began to cry.

She quickly stopped herself, getting up awkwardly and leaning heavily on her cane as she moved to the fireplace, her back to him.

"Why don't you tell me what this is really about?" he suggested, determined not to be swayed by her tears.

"You're right, of course." She didn't turn around as she brushed at the tears, her back ramrod straight. "I have reason to believe that one of you saw something from the window up there. I thought if you had that you'd tell me. After all these years I'd assumed there would be no reason for any of you to keep the secret any longer. I foolishly assumed that one of you would want the truth to come out."

Her candor surprised him as much as her apology and her tears had. He didn't know what to say.

"I know it's possible that I'm wrong," she said, making it sound as if she didn't believe it. "Maybe none of you saw Trace being murdered." She turned to face him. "You see now why it is so important that I find out the truth. I don't believe the killer acted alone. I'm basing that assumption on where Trace was killed—within sight of the ranch. The killer got him to that spot, I believe, for a good reason. Because someone else was watching from the ranch that day. I believe that person didn't know that you children were in that third-floor room with a pair of binoculars."

Jack was stunned. "You're saying you think someone from the family was involved in Trace's murder?"

"Yes, I do."

So that was what this was about. He couldn't believe what he was hearing, and yet even as a small child he was aware of the jealousy among the siblings.

"I intend to find out who that person is if it takes my last dying breath."

Jack stared at her. "That's why you invited us all back."

She nodded. "I would be a foolish old woman to think that I could make up for the past at this late date." She shook her head. "I won't rest until I find out the truth. Will you help me?" Her voice broke and he felt something break in him, as well.

He reached inside himself for all the hatred he'd carried for this woman the past twenty-seven years, but that fire that had consumed him for so long had burned down to only a handful of red-hot embers.

His words surprised him, since he didn't feel he owed this woman anything given the hell she'd put his parents through. "We were in the room that morning."

His grandmother slumped down onto the hearth.

"We'd heard stories about the room and wanted to see it."

"Whose idea was it to go up there?" she asked in a voice fraught with emotion.

"I don't recall. All the adults were busy with Trace's birthday preparations for that afternoon."

Pepper's eyes shone brightly in the firelight as if remembering.

"I'm sorry, but I didn't see anything." He'd been busy reading what had been scratched into the walls.

Her disappointment was palpable. "Did one of your cousins have a pair of small binoculars?"

He felt a start as he remembered the binoculars.

"Which cousin?" she asked, witnessing his reaction.

"I...I really don't recall." He'd been distracted. By the writing on the walls. And the girl. Jack had wondered where she'd come from and why he hadn't seen her before. He gathered she shouldn't be there, that she'd sneaked in, ridden over from the only close ranch nearby, the McCormick Ranch. He'd forgotten until now, but there'd been another girl with her, a younger girl who they all ignored.

"I remember Cordell and Cyrus fighting over the binoculars." Showing off for the older girl. "I honestly can't remember which one of them ended up with the binoculars."

Jack wondered what his grandmother would say if he told her about the girls? He wasn't sure what held him back. Certainly not loyalty to his cousins or their friends. He wasn't even sure why he'd told his grandmother what he had. Just for a moment there, he'd felt sorry for her, he supposed.

She nodded slowly, as if sensing he was holding back something. "I would think that if anyone saw their uncle being murdered, that boy would have had a reaction. He might not have told me, but I would think he'd have told his cohorts."

"You have to remember, I was just the nanny's kid," Jack said, digging up some of that old pain to remind himself why he was here. "My so-called cousins weren't all that fond of me. So if they had secrets, they kept them to themselves."

She rose, but with effort. He started to help her, but she waved his hand away. "If you should think of anything that might help me..."

Did she really think he was here to help her?

He was glad when his grandmother called it a night and he could go look for Josey. He was relieved to find her alone, sitting in the tire swing under one of the massive cottonwood trees. A rain squall had blown through, but it was dry under the trees. He loved the smell after a rain almost as much as he loved the scent of Josey's damp hair.

"You all right?" Jack asked, as he gave her a push. The rope tied to the limb overhead creaked loudly.

Josey jumped off and turned as if he'd scared her.

He remembered the rope burn on her neck and mentally kicked himself for being so stupid. "I'm sorry, I—"

"No, it's just that I get motion sickness on swings."

Right. "Dinner was fun," he said sarcastically, to change the subject.

"Wasn't it." She stepped from under the canopy of cottonwood limbs and turned her face upward. "Have you ever seen so many stars?"

"You don't see many where you live?"

She didn't look at him. "No. I live in the city."

He found the Big Dipper, one of the few constellations he knew. He wanted to know more about Josey, but he knew better than to ask. Whoever had hurt her made her afraid to trust. He could understand that.

"HOW DID YOUR TALK GO with your grandmother?" Josey asked, afraid he was about to question her.

"She talked a lot about Trace, my uncle who was murdered."

"What was that she asked yesterday about some room that is off-limits?" Josey asked.

He turned to look back at the house and pointed. The room was barely visible from this angle, as it was on the far wing set back against the hillside—the wing that had been boarded up. It was an odd wing, she noticed. If had been built back into the side of a hill and appeared to be much older than the original structure. As an afterthought, a room had been added near the back.

"That's the room?" she asked.

"That's it."

"What's in it?"

"Nothing. A window." He shook his head. "Nothing else. It's soundproof."

"Soundproof?" She realized he'd been in the room, just as his grandmother had suspected. "Why is whether or not you were in the room such a big deal to your grandmother?"

Jack looked like he wished she hadn't asked. "Between you and me? She thinks one of us might have seen my uncle Trace murdered." He nodded at her surprised reaction. "There were a pair of binoculars in the room. I never touched them, but the others were looking through them. She thinks one of them witnessed the murder. The alleged murderer confessed, but was killed. My grandmother believes there was an accomplice, someone from the family, and that's why Trace was murdered within sight of the ranch."

"Well, if one of you kids had seen something, wouldn't you have told?"

"Maybe the kid did, and maybe whoever he told was the accomplice."

"That's horrible."

"It's also why she is getting us all back here, to interrogate us individually to get at the truth."

Josey jumped as she realized Enid was standing in the shadows off to the side.

"I guess you didn't hear me call to you," Enid said, stepping toward them. "I wanted to see if there was anything I could get you before I turned in."

"No," Josey and Jack said in unison.

"Well, fine then," the housekeeper said. She turned on her heel and headed for the house.

"That woman is the worst eavesdropper I've ever come across," Josey whispered. "I don't trust her."

"Me, either."

"The way she treats your grandmother, it makes me wonder."

Jack nodded solemnly. "It's almost as if she and her husband have something on Pepper, isn't it?"

Josey realized she was getting chilly. She started to head for the house when Jack touched her arm, stopping her.

"Thank you for being here. I mean that. No matter what, I'm not sorry."

"I hope you never are," she said, knowing he would be soon enough as they walked back to the house and their bedroom. Jack curled up in his chair. Josey thought she'd never be able to sleep, but, still tired from the long horseback ride that day, she dropped right off.

JACK WOKE TO A SCREAM. He bolted upright in the chair, momentarily confused. The scream was coming from the bed.

He shot to his feet and stumbled in the dark over to the bed. "Josey." He shook her gently, feeling the perspiration on her bare arm. "Josey," he said, shaking her more forcefully.

The scream caught in her throat. She jerked away, coming up fighting. She swung at him, both arms flailing wildly.

"Josey!" he cried, grabbing her arms and pinning her down. "It's me, Jack. You were having a bad dream." He released one of her wrists to snap on the light beside the bed.

She squirmed under him, then seemed to focus on him. He felt the fight go out of her, but her face was still etched in fear and she was trembling under him, her body soaked in sweat.

He let go of her other wrist and eased off of her, sitting up on the edge of the bed next to her. He could hear her gasping for breath.

"That must have been some dream," he said quietly, thinking of the rope burn on her neck. Whatever had happened to her was enough to give anyone nightmares.

"I'm okay now."

He wasn't sure if she was trying to convince him or herself. "If you want to talk about it…" He reached over to push a lock of dank hair back from her face.

"I can't even remember what it was about." She shifted her gaze away.

"That's good," he said, going along with the lie. He stood. "If you want I can leave the light on."

She shook her head. "I'm sorry I woke you."

"No problem." He doubted he'd be able to go back to sleep, but he returned to his chair, glad Enid had put them at the end of the wing away from everyone, so no one else heard the screams.

Josey turned out the light. He heard her lie back down. The darkness settled in. He listened to her breathe and thought about how a man would go about killing a bastard like the one who'd given Josey such horrible nightmares.

He also thought about how a man might go about keeping Josey in his life.

It was while he was eating in the kitchen at the house at Mobridge that RJ spotted the phone hanging on the wall.

He'd had to break into the house and had been surprised to find that it appeared someone still lived here.

That was good and bad. The good part was that they weren't home and he'd been able to find some clean clothes, a warm coat, boots that were only a little too big and some drugs to tide him over.

He'd also been able to find food. Not much in the refrigerator so he suspected they'd gone into town to shop. He made himself some soup, ate the canned meat straight from the can along with the canned peaches he'd found, leaving the empty containers on the table. It wasn't like they wouldn't figure out someone had been here.

It appeared a man and woman lived in the house, both older from the clothing he'd found. He'd gone through the woman's jewelry box. Nothing worth stealing. But he'd managed to scare up almost a hundred dollars from a cookie jar in the kitchen and the man's sock drawer.

He got up, searched around for a phone book and finally found one in a drawer. It had doodles all over the front along with an assortment of numbers.

He pulled a chair over so he could sit and opened the phone book to Whitehorse, the town up the road in the direction the yellow Cadillac convertible had been heading when the driver picked up Josey. There were only a few pages, so it didn't take long to find the numbers he needed. He started with gas stations. With towns so few and far between up here, the driver of the Cadillac would have filled up before going any farther up the road.

Three gas stations. He called each, coming up with a story about trying to find his brother-in-law. The clerks were all friendly, that small-town trust that he had a growing appreciation for with each call.

No luck there. He began to call the motels on the chance that the Caddie driver had dropped Josey at one.

He got lucky on his fifth call.

"I remember seeing a yellow Cadillac," a clerk at one of the motels told him.

RJ tried not to sound too excited. "There at the motel?"

"No, over in front of the clothing store."

RJ frowned. "You saw the guy driving it? Was there a woman with him?"

"No. Just a man when I saw him and the car."

He was disappointed. Maybe the guy had already gotten rid of Josey. It just seemed odd the guy would be shopping for clothing, unless...

That damned Josey. She probably cried on the guy's shoulder and suckered him in. RJ could understand being smitten with her. She was one good-looking woman. He'd wanted her himself.

Should have taken her, too, when he had the chance. He'd planned to, but Celeste had thrown a fit when he suggested the three of them get together. Once he'd given Celeste that engagement ring she was no fun anymore.

So let's say Josey got the driver of the Cadillac to buy her clothes. Then what else would she get him to do for her?

He tried the last motel, convinced he'd find Josey curled up watching television and thinking she'd gotten away.

"I saw the car," the male clerk said. "Sweet. One of those vintage restored jobs."

RJ couldn't have cared less about the work done on the Caddie. "So she's staying there at the motel?"

"The woman with him? No." The guy sounded confused. "I saw the *car* when I was getting gas at Packy's."

That was one of the numbers he'd already called. "Did you happen to notice if there was a woman with him? A woman with long, curly, reddish-blond hair, good-looking?"

The clerk had chuckled. "Good-looking, but she had short, curly, dark hair. And she wasn't with him then. I saw her in the car later."

"Wait a minute. So he didn't have her with him at the gas station, but you saw him with this woman later?"

"That's right. I passed the Cadillac. The cowboy was driving and the woman was in the passenger seat. I didn't get a really good look at her. She was kind of slumped down in the seat. But I saw she had short, curly, dark hair."

What? Slumped down in the seat? The answer came in a rush. Josey had changed her appearance. He wasn't sure how or when, but that had to be the explanation.

"Did you see which way they went when he drove out of town?"

"South."

"South?" Why would the driver go back the way he'd come? "On Highway 191 toward the river?"

"No, they took the Sun Prairie road. I was thinking I wouldn't take a car like that down that road."

RJ could only be thankful the cowboy hadn't been driving some nondescript sedan or this clerk would have never noticed him. "What's down that road besides Sun Prairie?"

The clerk laughed. "Well, there are some ranches, Fort Peck Reservoir, but they didn't look dressed for fishing. Mostly there's just a whole lot of open country."

RJ rubbed his temples. His head felt like it might explode. "So there is no way of knowing where he was going."

"Well, there wouldn't have been if he hadn't asked

me for directions when we were both getting gas in our rigs."

This clerk was on RJ's last nerve, plucking it like an out-of-tune guitar string. If this discussion had been in person, that jackass would be breathing his last breath shortly. *"Directions?"*

"To the Winchester Ranch. Didn't I mention that?"

Chapter Eight

Josey woke a little after one in the morning to find Jack's chair empty.

She sat up, listening. A breeze stirred the limbs of the large cottonwood tree outside the window. Shadows played on the bedroom floor, the curtains billowing in and out like breath.

Where was Jack? She slipped out of bed and went to the window. For a moment, she didn't see him. But just as he had the night before, he moved stealthily along the edge of darkness, staying to the deep shadows. He was headed like before toward the closed wing of the lodge.

She frowned and realized it was time she found out what her "husband" was up to. She feared that, whatever it was, if his grandmother found out it would get them kicked off the ranch. She wasn't about to admit that she was worried about Jack.

Grabbing the robe Jack had bought her, she shrugged into it, failing to talk herself out of what she was about to do.

At her door, she listened. No sound. Opening it, she crept out, carrying her cowboy boots. At the top of the stairs, she stopped. A dim light shone downstairs. It seemed to be coming from the kitchen.

Josey listened but hearing no sound tiptoed down the stairs to the front door. Easing it open, she stepped out, closing it behind her.

She hesitated on the front step to pull on her boots. Then she followed the same path Jack had taken, keeping to the shadows until she reached the far wing of the lodge.

It was an odd wing, she noticed. It had been built back into the side of a hill and appeared to be much older than the original structure. The doors and windows had been boarded up, but someone—Jack?—had removed the boards from the doorway.

The breeze picked up, the door blowing open a little wider as she stepped into the darkness of the boarded-up wing. The air was much colder in here and smelled musky, as if the wing had been closed up for some time.

Josey waited for her eyes to adjust to the darkness. She didn't move, hardly breathed as she listened. The only light bled in from the doorway. She'd left the door open, thinking it might be the only way she could find her way back.

At first she heard nothing but the sound of the breeze in the trees outside. Then her ears picked up a fainter sound coming from inside, a scratching noise that could have been mice. Or something larger.

She hesitated. Was it that important she find out what Jack was up to?

The answer was yes, she realized. She moved toward the noise, feeling her way along the dark hallway until she saw the shaft of light coming from under one of the doors.

Mice didn't carry flashlights, she told herself. She moved cautiously forward, stopping in front of the door. She listened to the scratching sound for a moment before she tried the cold knob.

It turned in her hand.

She took a breath. Was she sure she really wanted to know Jack's secrets? She eased the door open a few inches.

In the glow of his flashlight resting on one of the shelves, Josey saw Jack standing in front of a rock wall. Jack had a crowbar in his hand and was scraping mortar from between the stones.

The room appeared to be a root cellar with rows of shelves. There were dozens of old jars covered with dust, their contents blackened with age.

Jack worked feverishly, as if desperate to see what was on the other side of that wall.

Josey only had a moment to wonder about what she was seeing when a door slammed down the hall.

JACK FROZE, all his instincts on alert. Heavy footfalls echoed down the hall. The hall light flashed on. He swore under his breath and grabbed the flashlight, snapping it off as he turned to look toward the door.

The door was open. A figure was framed there. His heart caught in his throat. He knew that particular figure anywhere. Josey, dressed in only a robe and cowboy boots.

He started to take a step toward her, but she motioned him back as the heavy footfalls grew louder. Jack sank back into the dark shadows of the room, but there was no escape. He was caught. And so was Josey.

"What the hell are you doing in here?" boomed Alfred Hoagland's easily recognizable, raspy old voice. Through the doorway, Jack saw Alfred grab Josey by the arm.

Without a thought, he stepped toward the door, going to her rescue.

A giggle, high and sweet like a child's stopped him cold. *What the hell?* It took Jack a moment to realize it had come out of Josey.

"Are you daft?" Alfred demanded, letting go of her and stumbling back.

Josey seemed to come awake with surprise. She stumbled back into the wall, closing the door partway as she caught herself. "What…where am I?" She sounded both surprised and scared.

"Something wrong with you?" Alfred demanded, sounding a little afraid himself.

Josey let out a sob. "I can't have been sleepwalking again." She began to cry, covering her face with her hands. Jack had seen her cry and wasn't fooled.

Alfred cleared his voice, visibly uncomfortable. "You should get back to bed."

"I don't know where—"

Alfred let out a curse. "I'll take you." Jack could hear him grumbling to himself all the way down the hall as he led Josey out.

Jack waited until he heard the door close before he turned on his flashlight again. He couldn't chance that Alfred might get suspicious and come back. Taking some of the boards from the cellar shelving, he covered the spot where he'd been working. With luck, Alfred wouldn't notice if he did come back.

Jack knew he had Josey to thank for covering for him tonight, but he was furious with her. She'd taken a hell of a chance. She had no idea how much danger she'd put herself in.

As angry as he was at her for following him and butting into his business, he was also grateful and more than a little awed. Who was this amazing woman? It made him wonder what he saved her from on the highway. Had she felt she owed him? Well, they were even. He'd make sure she wasn't that foolhardy again.

But even as he thought it, he realized his aunt was apparently right about one thing. He and Josey were definitely a pair.

JOSEY HAD BEEN IN BED when Jack returned to the room. She pretended to be asleep, listening to him slip in and undress in the pitch blackness of the room.

Finally, he settled into the large chair.

She lay awake, listening to his breathing, knowing he, too, was still awake and just feet from her. She thought about rolling over and offering to share the bed with him. For the first time since they'd gotten "married," she felt they really were in this together.

But she remained mute, not daring to say the words because she knew right at that moment she was feeling scared and alone and would have given anything just to be held in his strong arms.

She knew, too, what would happen if she invited him into her bed.

"Josey?"

She froze, then said quietly, "Yes?"

"Don't ever follow me again."

She lay perfectly still, hearing the anger in his words and feeling her own fury race through her veins like liquid flames. She'd saved the bastard's bacon. "No need to thank me," she said sarcastically.

"We both have our secrets. Stay out of mine and I'll stay out of yours."

In the darkness, she touched the rope burn on her neck and felt the sting of tears. Sleep finally came as a godsend.

RJ DIPPED HIS FINGERS into the salve and touched it to his shoulder, grimacing with pain. He glared into the cheap mirror as if Josey was on the other side, relishing at the thought of the pain he would heap on her.

"I'm coming for you, bitch, and when I find you I'm going to hurt you in ways you never dreamed."

He opened one of the containers of prescription pills he'd found in the medicine cabinet. All of the pills were at least a year old, but if he took enough of them, he might be able to numb the pain, if not kill any infection.

Downing the pills, he took a drink and listened.

He felt better. His vision had cleared some and if he'd had a concussion, it seemed to be getting better. He'd turned on the radio, but hadn't heard any news, so he figured no news was good news.

Josey was smart. If he was right, she'd conned the driver of the Cadillac and was now on the Winchester Ranch miles from town. Hard to find, was what the clerk had said when RJ had made him give him the same directions he'd given the Cadillac driver.

Yeah, not that hard to find. He just hoped she

stayed put. He figured she would. She'd feel safe. Her mistake.

He wanted to go after her right now. No holds barred. But even in his dazed state, he knew that would be stupid.

First, he had to take care of himself. Get his strength back, patch up his wound. Hell, he wasn't going anywhere without a vehicle.

Josey always seemed to land on her feet. He hadn't been worried about her going to the cops—not with a murder rap hanging over her. She knew what would happen to her mother if she ended up behind bars. The thought made him frown. She had the money in the backpack. Would she try to get her mother moved out of the rest home his father had stuck her in?

Hell, yes. He stormed out of the bathroom, picked up the kitchen phone and called the nursing home.

"Just wanted to check on Ella Vanderliner. I mean Ella Evans," he said, when the night nurse answered.

"I'm sure she's asleep. May I ask who's calling?"

"Good. So she's still there?"

"I'm sorry, I didn't catch your name."

He hung up. Maybe he'd been wrong about Josey. Maybe her first thought had been to save her own skin without any thought to her mother.

He glanced in the bedroom at the soft-looking bed and thought about curling up for a while, but knew he couldn't chance it.

He'd gotten almost everything he'd needed here and he didn't want to push his luck. Now he just needed wheels. Unfortunately, all he'd found around this place was some old, broken-down, rusted farm equipment. No vehicle he could steal.

That meant he'd have to hit the road and hope someone stopped to give him a ride. But first he'd find a place to get some sleep in the pine trees again. His head would be clearer in the morning.

He wandered back into the bathroom, pocketed all the pills and a large bottle of aspirin. Pulling on the stolen coat, he took one last look around the kitchen, found some stale cookies and left Mobridge behind.

THE NEXT MORNING Josey woke to find Jack standing on the small balcony outside their room. He looked as if he had the weight of the world on his shoulders. For so long, she'd been so involved in her own problems that she'd been blind to anyone else's. That was what had gotten her into this trouble. Had she been paying attention—

She slid out of bed, wrapping her robe around her, and stepped out on the balcony next to him. Without giving it any thought, she put her arm around Jack as she joined him.

He glanced over at her, his smile shy, apologetic. "I'm sorry I snapped at you last night when I should have thanked you. But I was upset. You shouldn't have followed me."

She looked over at him, her eyes narrowing. "You mean the way you shouldn't have untied my scarf?"

He had the good sense to look chastised. "I wanted to help you."

"And why do you think I followed you last night?"

His gaze locked with hers. "You shouldn't be worrying about me. You have enough—"

"You can tell me what you're after," she said, lowering her voice. "I'll help you. You helped me by bringing me here." He started to argue the point. "Don't even bother to tell me you didn't know I was in some kind of trouble."

He smiled at her and touched her face. "Still," he said, shaking his head, "it's probably better that we don't know everything about each other."

His words cut like a knife, even though she agreed with him. They both had dark secrets, and yet living here pretending to be lovers was another kind of hell.

She pushed off the balcony railing and into the cool darkness of the bedroom, only to stop short at the sight of Enid standing in the middle of the room holding a stack of clean towels.

"I didn't think anyone was here," she said. Her expression left no doubt in Josey's mind that she'd heard everything.

JACK MENTALLY KICKED HIMSELF at the hurt expression on Josey's face as she'd left him on the balcony.

A moment later, he heard Enid's voice and swore. That damned sneaky woman. She'd probably heard everything. His fault. He should have been more careful.

Enid would take what she'd heard to his grandmother, sure as the devil.

But with a start, he realized he didn't care. Let her run to Pepper. Maybe it would be better if Pepper sent him packing. Hadn't he always known he might leave here empty-handed?

The bedroom door closed behind Enid, and he saw Josey standing in the middle of the room looking worried over what the woman had overheard. A wave of desire washed over him so strong, he thought it might drown him.

"She heard everything," Josey said, as he stepped into the bedroom, closing the French doors behind him.

He nodded, realizing he would have only one regret if he had to leave here—and it had nothing to do with what was or wasn't behind that rock wall in the closed wing.

"We should get down to breakfast," he said, his voice thick with emotion.

She didn't move as he stepped deeper into the room. "I think I'll skip breakfast," she said.

He started to talk her out of it, hating the thought of eating alone with just his grandmother and his aunt. But he saw the stubborn determination in the set of her jaw and decided to let it go.

They'd reached an impasse.

"I think I'll go for a horseback ride. Would you like—"

"No, thank you. I'll just stay in my room and read. I have a headache." Her words made it clear who'd given it to her.

"Should I have Enid send you up something to eat?"

Josey gave him a look of warning.

"I'll tell her not to disturb you, then." He stood for a moment, wanting to say all the things he felt, but unable to find the words. It was one thing to pretend they were husband and wife. It was another to get too close, and yet something like metal to magnet drew him to her. He wanted this woman. And not just for a week.

He had to fight every muscle within him not to reach for her.

As he descended the stairs, he found his grandmother waiting for him and groaned inwardly. Could this morning get any worse?

"Jack, may I speak with you?" Pepper led the way down to the parlor before he could answer.

The moment he stepped into the room, closing the door behind him as his grandmother instructed, she asked, "Why did you come here?"

Enid hadn't wasted any time. "Because you invited me and I wanted to see the ranch again."

His honest answer seemed to surprise his grandmother, who raised a brow. "I know you blame me for your unhappy childhood."

"My childhood wasn't unhappy."

"I kept your father from marrying your mother."

"Only until I was six. My father was an alcoholic and my mother spent her life trying to save him. Worse things happen to kids." He thought of his grandmother's children, that awful room on the third floor and what he'd seen scratched into the walls.

"I'm no fool," she snapped. "I know you want something from me, but I don't think it's my money."

As Josey said, the woman was sharp. "I have my own money, so it seems I came here to enjoy the ranch." He got to his feet. "Speaking of that, I'm going for a horseback ride."

"Alone?"

"Josey is resting. Please tell Enid she doesn't want to be disturbed."

Another raised brow. "Enid seemed to think that the two of you are going your separate ways when your week here is up."

"Enid should mind her own business." He saw that his grandmother had no intention of letting him leave it at that and sighed. "Josey and I, well, we think we might have acted in haste. Probably a little time apart would be good after we leave here," he said honestly.

Pepper's eyes narrowed, but when she spoke she said, "Enjoy your horseback ride. Don't go too far alone."

"Yes, I wouldn't want what happened to my grandfather to happen to me," he said, and saw his grandmother's expression darken.

PEPPER TOLD HERSELF she didn't care one way or the other about Jack and Josey's marriage, and yet she found herself climbing the stairs to the far wing. She'd noticed there was trouble between the two of them, but things seemed to have been a little better after their horseback ride yesterday.

Now, though, something seemed to have happened to drive them apart again. It seemed odd to her that Jack would go off on a horseback ride by himself. It was the first time he'd left Josey alone.

"Jack said you were resting, but I wanted to check on you," she said when Josey answered her knock.

The young woman looked uncomfortable.

"He's gone for a horseback ride. I thought you and I might…" She looked past Josey into the bedroom. *Her* bedroom when Call was alive.

"Would you like to come in?" Josey asked with obvious reluctance.

Pepper stepped into the room, fighting off the memories that assailed her. She and Call had shared this room from the first night she'd come to the ranch. Had she ever been happy?

Yes, at first she'd been deliriously happy. Naive, foolish, blind with love, but happy. It had lasted at least a week. Maybe even a month before she'd realized what a controlling bastard she'd married.

And yet she'd stayed, believing that he would change. She silently scoffed at the thought now. There'd been a time when she really believed that love could conquer all. Why else had she not only stayed with him but also had five children with him?

"Would you like to sit down?" Josey offered.

Pepper smiled at the young woman. She was kind and thoughtful, clearly from a good family.

"Thank you, I think that would be nice." She took one of the chairs, noticing as Josey removed a folded blanket and pillow from the other chair.

Josey must have seen her expression and smiled ruefully. "I'm sure you've heard that Jack and I have been having our problems."

"Enid is a terrible old busybody," Pepper said, anxiously anticipating the day she would be able to get rid of the woman for good. Impulsively, she reached over and took Josey's hand. "I know you and Jack aren't legally married."

Josey opened her mouth as if to explain, but Pepper waved her off. "Jack thinks I'm an old fool. Of course I had my lawyer investigate. I like to know who is sleeping under my roof."

"I feel I should apologize for letting you believe—"

"Oh, don't look so aghast. I like you. I was truly sorry to find out the two of you *weren't* married. You're good for Jack, and from what I've seen, he's good for you, as well."

JOSEY DIDN'T KNOW what to say. She had to admit that Pepper Winchester had caught her completely off guard.

"Are you shocked that I'm not upset? Or that I actually care for my grandson?"

Again the woman had caught her flat-footed. Before Josey could speak, Pepper laughed, easing the tension in the room.

"I am capable of love and caring. I like Jack. I'm sorry I hurt him and his mother. But there is nothing I can do about that. You live to be this old, you, too, will have regrets. I unfortunately have more than my share."

"You are definitely a surprise," Josey finally said, relaxing a little.

Pepper smiled at that. "I just remember what it's like to be in love."

Josey started to protest that she wasn't in love with Jack, but stopped herself. Even if she and Jack weren't legally married, they were still supposed to be in love. And she did care about Jack. Too much.

"Jack seems to think that the reason you're asking your family back to the ranch is because you're not satisfied with the results of your son's murder investigation," Josey said, needing to change the subject.

"That's true."

"I thought someone confessed."

"Yes. Unfortunately, that person is dead, and I have reason to believe that there was a second person involved. I have no proof."

"You think Jack knows something?"

Pepper smiled secretively. "I guess time will tell. If there is any chance that the person responsible for

Trace's death hasn't been brought to justice…" She shook her head. "It's something I need settled before I die."

"I can't believe it would be someone in your family."

"I've made a lot of mistakes in my life, but my greatest ones were with my children. Their father was a harsh disciplinarian. Too harsh. I didn't protect the older ones. But when Trace was born…" She cleared her throat.

"Would you like some water?" Josey asked. Pepper nodded, and she stood and went into the bathroom, returning with a glass of cold water.

"I should have stopped Call sooner," Pepper said, after taking a sip. "I should have done so many things differently. By then my older children had no respect for me, and in my guilt I avoided them. That rift grew wider as Trace became my life, the only part I cared about."

Josey wondered why Jack's grandmother was confessing all this to her. Just minutes before she'd opened the door to Pepper, she'd promised herself that she wasn't going to get any more involved with this family. In fact, she'd been thinking that the best thing she could do was to make an excuse to leave sooner.

"If one of my older children had anything to do with Trace's death, then I am to blame for it." Pepper nodded, tears in her eyes. "But I still want justice and I will still get it."

Josey felt a chill at the woman's words as Pepper set down the glass on the end table and rose, picking up her cane.

"Thank you for listening to an old woman ramble,"

she said, seeming embarrassed. "I hope you don't think ill of me."

"No," Josey said. As she rose to escort Pepper out, she thought of her own father. He would have killed for her. He also would have demanded justice had anything happened to her. But he was gone, and there was no one to protect her or see that justice was done.

"Please don't give up on Jack," Pepper said. "He needs you. I don't think he realizes how much. He prides himself on his independence and taking on the world alone—but then you are a lot like that yourself, aren't you?"

Josey was startled that Pepper had realized that about her. "Sometimes we have to take on things alone because there isn't anyone else," she said, echoing her earlier thoughts.

"But you aren't alone anymore. You have Jack."

"Yes," she said, feeling guilty at how wrong Pepper was about that.

Chapter Nine

McCall had known that once the news hit the radio and newspaper the calls would start coming in. Most of them were from residents who'd seen someone suspicious hanging around the alley, heard a noise out back or thought someone had been in their house.

Her deputies were running themselves ragged checking on suspicious characters, only to find the suspect was a relative of a neighbor or nothing at all.

When she took the call from the dispatcher she was expecting just another bad lead.

"It's Frank Hanover down at Mobridge," a man said. "We just got home from Billings and found our house has been broken into."

"What's missing?" McCall asked, thinking Mobridge was near the Missouri River, near the crime scene.

"Clothes, some of my shirts and pants, a coat, as far as I can tell. Cleaned all the drugs out of the medicine cabinet, ate some food and left a mess."

She sat up straighter, remembering the house at Mobridge. It was back off the road, no other houses around.

"Took a pair of my boots," Frank was saying.

"What size do you wear?" she asked.

"Eleven." He seemed to hesitate. "Is that important?"

It was to her. Ray Allan Evans Jr. wore a size 10½ loafer. He could make do with a pair of size 11 cowboy boots real easy. "What else was taken?"

"About a hundred dollars in cash, the wife and I estimate. That's all that we've found missing so far."

"Did he take one of your vehicles?"

"Weren't none to take," Frank said.

So RJ was still on foot. "I'm sending a deputy. Please try not to touch anything that the intruder left. You said he made a mess in the kitchen? Please leave it."

"He used our phone, looks like since he left the phone book out and a chair pulled up to it. Probably ran up our long distance bill," Frank grumbled.

"What's your number out there?" McCall asked, and wrote it down. As soon as she hung up, she called the phone company and asked for the phone log on recently dialed numbers.

"I'm sorry, but we're going to need a warrant to do that or permission from the customer. We'll need those in writing. You're welcome to fax them to us. That would speed things up."

McCall cursed under her breath. "I'll get back to you." She then called Frank Hanover back, then called a deputy who was still in the area and sent him over to pick up the written permission slip from the Hanovers.

She wanted to know if Frank Hanover was right and RJ had called someone. She needed to know where he was headed. She'd called in extra officers to help search the area near Mobridge, even though she suspected he was long gone.

He would be looking to steal a vehicle. It was just

a matter of time before he found one. She just prayed that no one would be driving it.

RJ DIDN'T KNOW how long he'd been walking up the dirt road when he heard the sound of an engine.

At first he thought he was hallucinating. It had been so long, and he'd been straining so hard to hear one. Praying for one, if he could call it praying. More like wishing on a curse.

He turned and saw what appeared to be a dark-colored pickup headed in his direction. RJ swallowed, his throat dry as he stuck out his thumb.

He'd cleaned up at the house, but he knew he still looked pretty rough. He feared no one would stop for him, so he was surprised when the driver slowed, then braked to a stop.

Sun glinted off the windshield, and it was a moment before he saw the lone driver, an old man dressed in a straw hat, flannel shirt and blue overalls.

He felt a wave of relief. One old farmer behind the wheel.

RJ would have shouted with glee if it wouldn't have made him look insane.

Both windows were already down on the old pickup. "Trouble?"

RJ stepped up to the open passenger-side window as dust settled around him. "Car broke down a good ways back by the river."

"You been walking this far in the wrong direction?" the farmer said with a laugh. "If you'd gone the other way, you have reached Highway 191 and gotten a ride a lot quicker than this."

As if RJ didn't know that. He'd opted for the less

traveled dirt road for a very good reason. The highway was too visible. He couldn't take the chance since he knew the California police would have put out an APB on him and Josey by now.

"Well, hop in. I can take you as far as Winifred, that's where I'm headed."

RJ couldn't have cared less where Winifred was as he opened the pickup's door and climbed in. He wouldn't be going that far anyway.

The pickup smelled of hay and possibly manure. It didn't matter. RJ couldn't believe how good it felt not to be walking. The boots he'd borrowed had rubbed blisters on both feet. He leaned back as the old farmer got the rig rolling and watched the land slip by, a sea of undulating green.

The farmer made several attempts to make conversation before turning on the radio. He picked up a station in Whitehorse, Montana, that, according to the farmer, played a polka of the day at noon.

The news came on. Ray tensed as he heard first Josephine Vanderliner's name and description, then his own, followed by a warning that both were considered armed and dangerous. He wished he was armed as the farmer reached under his seat and pulled out a tire iron.

JOSEY WATCHED THE SUN drop toward the dark outline of the Little Rockies in the distance. The spring day was hot and golden and held the promise of summer.

The prairie glowed under the heat. It was so beautiful and yet so alien. She wondered what this kind of isolation did to a person and thought of Pepper Winchester and the Hoaglands.

For the life of her she couldn't imagine what this

ranch must have been like when all the Winchesters had lived and worked here. Children running up and down the long hallways. The kitchen would have been bustling with activity, the whole ranch alive with sounds.

Josey wished she could have seen it. She sighed and looked to the road, anxious for Virginia to return from town. Earlier, she'd caught Virginia as she was leaving. The idea had come to her in a flash.

"Would you do me a huge favor?" Josey had asked her and seen the woman's irritation. "I just need to get some money wired to my mother's rest home."

Virginia's interest had picked up instantly. "Oh, honey, your mother's in a rest home? Why, she can't be very old. What's wrong with her?"

"Just give me a moment to get the money and the address." She'd run back up the stairs, telling herself this was the only way. No one knew Virginia. And it wasn't like involving Jack. Virginia couldn't get in trouble over this since she really was an innocent bystander.

Josey had dug through the stacks of hundreds, choosing bills free of blood. She'd already set up her mother's transfer, planning to move her mother from the horrible rest home where her stepfather had stuck her—to one where he couldn't find her.

Virginia's eyebrow had shot up when she saw the wad of money.

"I wasn't sure I could get a check cashed anywhere up here, and everything with Jack happened so fast..."

His aunt had pursed her lips in disapproval. "Marry in haste and... Well, you know." She seemed a little upset that Josey hadn't satisfied her curiosity about her mother.

"Here's the address. They're expecting the money. I can't thank you enough for doing this."

Virginia had left then, promising to bring her a receipt and let her know that the money had arrived.

Neither Virginia nor Jack had returned and it was getting late. Josey got more restless by the moment. Tired of watching for both of them, she turned away from the window and went into the bathroom to bathe before supper, wondering if Jack would be back by then.

Her bruises were healing. So was the rope burn on her neck. Soon she wouldn't have to wear the scarves. But she would have to disappear. As long as she was free, her mother should be safe.

She closed her eyes as she slid down into the warm water filled with bubbles. Once her mother was safe and she was sure nothing could change, then she would deal with the fact that she was wanted for murder and she had no way to prove her innocence.

She opened her eyes and climbed out of the tub, wishing she could go to the police and just get it over with. As she toweled herself and pulled on the bathrobe, she told herself that maybe if the police knew what had happened—

No, RJ was right. She would fry, and what would happen to her mother?

She thought about the rest of the bloody money in the armoire and felt nauseous as she opened the bathroom door and stepped out. Either way, she would never see her mother again, she thought, as she looked through her clothes for something to wear to supper.

"Are you all right?"

She jumped as Jack touched her shoulder. She hadn't heard him return.

He looked so concerned, she was filled with guilt for dragging him into this, even if it had been his idea. She'd only been thinking of herself. She hadn't considered the spot she was putting him in.

"You scared me."

"I'm sorry." He sounded as if he meant it. The last of the day's light shone on his face through the open French doors, accentuating the strong lines of his face. "Sorry about a lot of things."

"Sorry you brought me here?" She felt a little piece of her heart break off and fall.

"No," he said. "No, you're wrong about that. If I've been distant it's just because..." He raised his hand, signaling to her to wait a moment, then walked over and locked the bedroom door. "Enid won't be coming back in without us knowing it," he said, as he dragged a straight-back chair from the small desk in the corner and wedged it under the doorknob.

"Jack?" Josey said. He turned to her, and she saw the look in his eyes. She'd noticed that he seemed different after his ride. More relaxed. More like the Jack she'd met on the highway.

"You want the truth?" he asked.

She swallowed as he moved toward her.

"I think it's time I was honest with you. I've been pushing you away because if I don't..."

JOSEY'S GREEN EYES widened in alarm—and something that seemed to simmer on the back burner as he moved toward her, his gaze locked with hers.

It had always been so easy to lose himself in that sea of green. He stopped just inches from her, saw her eyes fire as he reached for her robe sash and slowly untied it.

"Do you have any idea what you're doing?" she asked, her voice breaking.

He chuckled. "It's been a while, but I think I remember how it goes."

She placed her hand over his to stop him, her eyes searching his. "Jack—"

He knew all the reasons they shouldn't take this pretend marriage any further than they had. Hell, he'd listed them at length on his long horseback ride today.

"I want you. That, Josey, is the truth." He looked into her eyes, then he gently pushed her hand away and untied the robe sash. It fell open to expose bare flesh.

He slipped his hands around her slim, bare waist and felt desire spread through him, a fire rushing through his veins.

His gaze still locked with hers, he inched his hands up to cup her full breasts in each palm. She let out a sound and arched against him. He felt her nipples harden against his palms.

Slowly, his hands moved upward. He eased the robe off her slim shoulders. It dropped to the floor, and for a moment he was taken aback at how beautiful she was.

"I want to make love to you," he whispered.

Josey let out a soft moan and he felt something give inside him. He'd never wanted anything the way he wanted this woman.

His palms skimmed over her small waist to her hips. Cupping her perfect derriere in both hands, he dragged her to him, no longer able to stand another moment without kissing her again.

Her lips parted as his mouth dropped to hers. He

heard her moan again and felt her working at the snaps of his Western shirt, and then his chest was pressed against her warm, full breasts, her nipples hard as stones, and he was carrying her to the canopied bed.

JOSEY WRAPPED THE ROBE around her and stepped to the window, the white sheer curtains billowing in on the evening breeze. She breathed in the unfamiliar scents as if only just now aware of them. Everything felt new and fresh, the day brighter. She hugged herself, smiling as she closed her eyes and turned her face up to the warmth of the sunset, reveling in the memory of making love with Jack.

Jack still lay on the bed behind her. She could feel his gaze on her. It heated her skin more than even the evening warmth. She would never forget the feel of his hands, his mouth, his body. His gentleness. His passion. He'd consumed her, filled her, fulfilled her.

"Come back to bed," he said softly. "We don't have much time. If we don't make an appearance at supper, I'm afraid there will be hell to pay."

She smiled to herself and was about to turn back when a flash of light caught her eye. The sun glinted off the bumper of a vehicle coming down the road toward them.

Josey froze, her pulse thundering in her ears.

"What is it?" Jack asked, sensing the sudden change in her. He pulled on his jeans and joined her on the balcony.

Her heart began to pound louder as she saw that there was something on top of the SUV roaring up the road. A light bar. And on the side of the vehicle a Sheriff's Department logo.

"It must be my cousin McCall Winchester," he said, as a woman with long, dark hair climbed out of the patrol car. Even from this distance Josey could tell she was wearing a sheriff's uniform.

"What do you think she wants?" Josey asked, fighting to keep the terror out of her voice. She'd thought she was safe here. That Jack was safe. She should never have involved him.

"My grandmother must have invited her for dinner," he said, as he drew Josey inside the bedroom and shut the French doors. "What's wrong?"

"Jack, I'm really not up to meeting her." She felt the heat of his gaze. He'd known she was in trouble. Now he knew it was with the law. "I should have told you—"

He touched a finger to her lips. "I'll take care of it." Jack's gaze locked with hers. "You're trembling. You should get back in bed."

"Jack—"

"It's going to be all right." He pulled her to him and kissed her. "You can meet my cousin some other time. Don't worry, I'll make apologies for you. I shouldn't have taken you on such a long horseback ride yesterday. I'd hate to think you're coming down with something."

She closed her eyes and wished they could just stay in this room forever. Become recluses just as his grandmother had done for twenty-seven years. No one had known for sure whether she was alive or dead. Nor had they cared.

She opened her eyes and grabbed for him as he started for the door. "I can't let you get in any deeper."

He took her in his arms, planted a kiss in her hair, then pulled back and smiled. "I'll be back as quick as I can. Lock the door behind me."

JACK LEFT JOSEY and went downstairs. He had known Josey was in trouble, but he'd just assumed it involved a man—not the law. As he descended the stairs, he had flashes of their lovemaking. He knew it had probably been a mistake, but even given what he now knew about his "wife," he couldn't regret it.

Enid opened the front door and Jack slowed on the stairs. He'd heard about McCall when the news had come about Trace Winchester's murder and the role Trace's daughter, a sheriff's deputy, had played in helping solve the crime—including almost getting herself killed.

So he'd been curious about his cousin the cop. He'd heard she'd been promoted to acting sheriff—their grandmother's doing, he would bet. Pepper Winchester might have been a recluse for the past twenty-seven years but she was still a force to be reckoned with, especially considering all the land she owned and the Winchester fortune. Which was surprising, given all the stories he'd heard about where that fortune had come from and at what cost.

He thought of the stories his mother had told him, and now he wondered how many of them were true. He had to remind himself that his mother had believed everything Angus Winchester had told her, and look where that had gotten her.

Still, he'd believed at least one of those stories was true. That's why he'd come here. Strange how long ago that seemed and, maybe more startling, how it had become less important.

McCall looked up as he came down the stairs. He couldn't hide his shock. She looked exactly like his grandmother had at that age.

She smiled at his surprise. "You must be Jack." She held out her hand. He stopped to shake it.

He found it amusing how wrong his grandmother had been. He recalled overhearing, when he was six, Pepper saying her son Trace had eloped with a local tramp who was lying through her teeth about the baby she was carrying being her son's. Clearly, Ruby Bates hadn't been lying. McCall was a Winchester.

"Oh, I see you two have met," Pepper said, appearing from down the hall. "Where is your wife?" she asked Jack.

"She isn't feeling well. I think she might have picked up a bug. I shouldn't have taken her on such a long horseback ride, as hot out as it was yesterday."

His grandmother looked suspicious. "McCall was looking forward to meeting her."

He turned his attention to the acting sheriff. "I'm sure you'll get to meet her when she's feeling better. It isn't like we're going anywhere for a while."

RJ TURNED OFF the first side road he came to. Now that he had a ride, all he could think about was sleeping in a real bed tonight.

His shoulder hurt like hell, and he worried that it was infected. Wouldn't that be a kicker if he died from a stupid flesh wound?

He felt himself coming down from the rush of killing the farmer. He'd been glad when the old fart had pulled out the tire iron. Taking it away from him had almost been too easy. He'd smacked him a couple times with it, then reached over and opened the old man's door, shoving him out before sliding over behind the wheel to stop the pickup.

Once he'd gotten rid of the body, his head ached again but he knew he had to start thinking more clearly.

The pickup was old and dark colored, like a zillion others in this part of Montana. But he did stop and smear some mud on the license plate. He could camp out somewhere, hide the pickup, but he was counting on the farmer's body not being found for a while.

Eventually someone would call the sheriff's department to notify them that the old guy was missing. But in the meantime, RJ decided to press his luck.

He would drive to Billings, the largest city in Montana, where he could get what he needed—and not be noticed. It was out of his way by a few hours, but he couldn't chance going into Whitehorse. Too small. People noticed outsiders in that kind of town.

He shoved the farmer's hat down on his head and drove toward Highway 191. Tonight he would break into a pharmacy and steal the drugs and medical supplies he needed. He would sleep in a motel room bed, charging the room to the credit card he'd found in the old guy's wallet, and he'd have a nice meal.

Eventually, the cops would track the expenditures. But he would make sure they never connected it to him. Or at least make sure they couldn't prove it. Later tonight he would ditch the pickup and get himself a new ride, one no one in Whitehorse would recognize. Then he'd see about getting himself a gun.

Chapter Ten

Move! Josey grabbed her clothes and quickly got dressed, her mind racing. She found her backpack and opened the armoire, dumping the old clothing out and reaching for the money. Just touching it made her sick to her stomach.

But she couldn't leave it here, and she knew the day would come when she would need it to hire herself a good lawyer. In the bathroom, she retrieved the gun and dropped it on top of the money in the backpack.

Her gaze fell over the room, stopping on the canopy bed and the rumpled sheets. Her heart broke at the memory of the two of them making love there earlier. She'd given herself to Jack completely, surrendering in a way she'd never thought possible. He'd been so gentle, so loving. She thought of the passion that had arced between them. Had she been a romantic, she would have said they were made for each other.

But she was a realist, and because of that she knew making love with him had been a mistake. She was a woman wanted by the law. How could she have been so foolish to fall for Jack?

The realization struck her like a train. She'd let herself fall in love with this cowboy from Wyoming. Now there would always be this empty place inside her heart that only Jack Winchester could fill.

She took one last glance around the room. All she knew was that she had to get out of here, get away, far away. Once she knew her mother was safe...

Josey jumped at the sound of an engine turning over. Rushing to the window, she saw the sheriff's department car pulling away. Her hammering heart began to slow, then took off again as she heard the tap at the door.

"Josey, it's me."

She rushed to the door and into Jack's arms. All her plans to escape, to run far away, to keep her distance from this man went out the window the moment she saw the smile on his face.

"My cousin just stopped by because my grandmother had been nagging her to," Jack said. "She's on some big case and couldn't stay but a minute. She was disappointed, though, that she didn't get to meet my wife."

Relief made her weak as Jack locked the door, swept her up in arms and carried her back to the bed.

"All I could think about was getting back to you," he whispered against her hair. His mouth found hers.

She tried to speak, but he smothered her words with kisses. As he began to make love to her, all reason left her. There was no other place she wanted to be but in Jack's arms.

PEPPER WATCHED HER GRANDDAUGHTER drive away. The pride she felt surprised her, as did the guilt. She wished she'd known McCall sooner. She'd lost twenty-seven years of McCall's life. Her own fault.

She brushed angrily at the sudden tears that blurred her eyes, surprised by them and these feelings. She hadn't believed for a moment that the baby Ruby Bates had been carrying was her son Trace's. Because she hadn't wanted to.

But the two had produced McCall, and there was little doubt she was a Winchester. She hadn't even needed to see the DNA test. The young woman looked just like Pepper had at that age.

Trace had been her baby, her undeniable favorite, and she'd been sick with worry because she knew she was losing him. He'd married Ruby Bates because she'd been pregnant. Or maybe because he really had loved her. Pepper had never really known. Trace was dead, and maybe even Ruby didn't know the truth.

Not that it mattered. They had produced McCall, and she made up for everything.

It still amazed her that McCall seemed to have forgiven her for her past sins, unlike her children and even her other grandchildren. McCall knew that she'd tried everything to get Trace to dump Ruby and come back to the ranch.

So maybe Trace had loved McCall's mother. Loved McCall even though she hadn't been born before he was murdered. After all, according to McCall, it had been her father's idea to name her after her grandfather Call.

She wiped her tears as the dust from McCall's patrol car settled over the wild landscape, hating these sentimental emotions and wondering if she should have just left well enough alone and died in her sleep without ever getting her family back to the ranch.

"Mother?"

She turned to see Virginia standing in the doorway.

She'd been so lost in thought, she hadn't heard her enter.

"I'm bored to tears. I'm going into town again. Can I get you anything?"

"No, but you should ask Enid if she needs any groceries, since you're going," Pepper said.

Virginia made a face. "She already gave me a long list. I hope to be back by supper. Enid wanted to know if you knew if Jack and his wife would be joining us. Apparently, they missed both breakfast and dinner."

A good sign, Pepper thought. "Tell Enid to plan on it. If they decide to skip another meal, that will be fine also."

Virginia didn't look happy about being asked to relay the message to Enid, but acquiesced. "Too bad Enid is such a horrible cook. I can't understand how you have survived eating her food all these years."

Her daughter had no idea.

As McCall drove back to Whitehorse, she thought about her relationship with her grandmother. She'd never even laid eyes on the woman until last month. But since that time her life had changed—and Pepper Winchester had had her hand in that.

She wasn't sure why she'd forgiven her grandmother for denying her existence for more than twenty-seven years. Maybe she saw herself in Pepper Winchester— and not just the fact that they resembled each other. Or maybe what had brought them together was the shared loss of a father and son. McCall had never gotten to know her father. Trace had been killed before she was born. Her grandmother's loss had been even greater because Trace had been her favorite, and losing him had made her lock herself away for the past twenty-seven years.

A call pulled McCall out of her reverie. "I've got Sharon Turnquist on the line. She says her husband is missing." Sharon farmed and ranched with her husband John south of the Breaks.

"Put her through."

"John left to go into Winifred and never got there," Sharon said, sounding worried and scared. "Neighbors are out looking for him, driving the road south, thinking he must have gone off somewhere along the way."

The Turnquist Ranch was a good fifteen miles from Mobridge on a narrow dirt road that wound through the rough badlands country. What were the chances this wasn't connected to Ray Allan Evans Jr.?

"I've got a deputy down that way," she said. "I'll have him help in the search. You let me know when you find him."

She hung up and called to make sure that the deputy she'd sent down to Mobridge had returned with a signed agreement from the Hanovers. Both had been faxed to the phone company, she was informed.

McCall hung up feeling antsy. She just hoped to hell that RJ hadn't stumbled across John Turnquist. She knew the elderly farmer and his wife. You couldn't ask for two nicer people.

Unfortunately, John was the kind of man who would stop and offer a ride to anyone walking along the road. This was rural Montana, where people still helped one another. Even strangers.

JACK AND JOSEY finally came up for air and realized they were both starving. They laughed and played in the huge clawfoot tub before getting dressed in time to go downstairs for supper.

There was an unspoken truce between them, Jack thought. It was as if they knew they didn't have much time together—although right now, feeling the way he did, he couldn't imagine a day without Josey in it.

He was surprised when Virginia was the one late for supper. She came into the lodge complaining about the road into Whitehorse, the dust, the distance, the rough road. She plopped down at the table, announcing she was starved as she distractedly thumbed through the newspaper she'd bought in town.

"Do you have to do that at the table during supper?" Pepper asked with no real heat behind it.

Jack had noticed that his grandmother didn't seem to be herself. She appeared even more distracted than even Virginia.

"I picked up the Whitehorse newspaper since everyone in town was talking about the front-page article," Virginia said, as if she hadn't heard her mother. "A car was found in the Missouri River south of town after a fisherman hooked into the body of a woman. You can't believe the rumors that are flying around town. What has everyone so worked up is a rumor that the woman was found with a noose around her neck. Someone had hung her!"

Josey's fork rattled to her plate.

Jack's gaze shot to Josey. All the color had drained from her face.

"Virginia!" her mother snapped. "We're *eating*."

"Why didn't McCall tell us about this?" Virginia demanded of her mother. "This must be the big case she is working on. Everyone is supposed to be on the lookout for possibly two individuals who might have been hitch-hiking from somewhere near the Fred Robinson Bridge on the Missouri River crossing."

Jack heard all the air rush from Josey's lips. Her fingers gripped the table as if she were on a ship tossed at sea.

"They believe the driver of the vehicle got away after the car went into the water and that both suspects are believed to be armed and dangerous!" Virginia said, scanning through the story. "Apparently, they are both wanted for questioning in a murder case in California. The photos of them aren't very good in grainy black-and-white."

Josey stumbled to her feet. "I'm sorry, I—" She rushed out.

Pepper threw down her napkin, silverware clattering, and shoved back her chair. "Don't you ever know when to shut up, Virginia? Go after her, Jack. That woman could be the best thing that ever happened to you. Don't be like your father."

Jack was already on his feet before his grandmother had even spoken. He'd been so shocked by the news Virginia had brought home, it had taken him a few moments to move. He snatched the newspaper from Virginia's fingers.

"Oh, God, you don't think she's pregnant already, do you?" he heard his aunt say as he rushed from the room.

THE CALL CAME IN late that evening from the deputy McCall had sent out to the Turnquist Ranch.

"One of the other ranchers spotted a body down in a gully," the deputy told her. "It's John Turnquist. I put in a call to the coroner. He's on his way out. Thought I'd better let you know. There's no sign of the pickup he was driving. His wallet's missing, as well. His wife said he didn't have much money in it, but did have several credit cards."

RJ. "Tell her not to cancel the credit cards just yet," McCall said. "We might be able to track him that way. We'll need numbers on the cards so we can work with the companies, and we're going to need a description of that pickup."

"There's something else," the deputy said. "Can't be sure until George gets here, but it looked like John was beaten with something before he was dumped out and rolled down into the gully."

She swore under her breath. "Well, at least now we know what Ray Allan Evans Jr. is driving. Let's find this bastard before he finds his next victim."

JOSEY RAN TO THEIR ROOM at the end of the empty wing, her heart pounding in her ears.

Celeste's body had been found. But the heart-stopping news: RJ was alive. He'd gotten away. She knew what that meant. He would be coming after her. Probably already was.

She stopped pacing to stand in the middle of the bedroom, her mind racing. She had to get out of here. She had to—

At the sound of the door opening behind her, she spun around.

"Talk to me," Jack said quietly, as he closed the door and locked it.

She shook her head and took a step back. "I need to get out of here."

"Josey, you have to tell me what all this has to do with you." His words were heavy with emotion as he put down the newspaper. "After what's happened between us, you owe me that."

She tried to swallow. Her stomach roiled. "I've already involved you. I can't—"

"Josey." He took a step to her, his big hands cupping her shoulders. "I can't help you if you don't tell me—"

"It's all too..." She waved a hand through the air, unable to even form words to describe what had happened to her. "You don't want any of this. Let me leave. Pretend you never picked me up on that highway."

"I can't do that." He sounded filled with anguish.

She stared at him in disbelief. "Aren't you just a little worried that I'm a murderer?"

His blue eyes lit with something akin to love as he took hold of the ends of the scarf around her neck and slowly began to untie it.

"Don't." The word came out a whisper.

"This is why I don't believe you're a killer," he said softly. "Someone did this to you. Just as someone did it to that woman they found."

She fought back the horrible memories. "You don't understand. You could be arrested for harboring a fugitive. Jack, everyone is looking for me, the police in California, the sheriff here in Montana, and..." Tears filled her eyes.

"And the person who hurt you. That's what has you so terrified." Jack thumbed at her tears, then kissed her. "But you're going to tell me because you know you can trust me."

She smiled at that. "The last man who told me to trust him almost killed me."

"I'm not that man."

No, Josey thought. Jack Winchester, whatever his secrets, was like no man she'd ever met. And right now, she suspected he might be the only person alive who'd believe her story.

AFTER BREAKING INTO a small older pharmacy and getting everything he needed, RJ had gone back to his motel and seen to his shoulder before going to sleep. He'd picked a Billings motel where he could park the pickup so the clerk couldn't see it. The clerk had been half-asleep when he'd checked in and hadn't paid any attention to him, anyway. He'd worn the hood up on the sweatshirt he'd taken from the Mobridge house just in case, though. No way could the man be able to make a positive ID of him.

He'd set his alarm for just after midnight and had come up with a way to get rid of all the evidence and the truck. Since hotwiring these damned new cars was next to impossible even if he knew how, he decided to take a more direct approach.

He drove around until he found a rundown bar on the south side of Billings. Then he crossed the river, and found an old abandoned farm house. Driving into the yard with his lights off, he parked the truck behind one of the out buildings.

He'd seen enough *CSI* to know exactly how arsonists set fires. With the pack of cigarettes he'd bought at a convenience mart and the extra gas in the back of the truck, he'd soaked the front seat and set the makeshift fuse.

He'd been about a half mile away, walking down the road, when the pickup blew. RJ smiled to himself as he walked the rest of the way to the bar. The back parking lot was cloaked in darkness. Ideal for what he had in mind.

The jukebox blared inside the bar, one of those serious drinkers' bars where patrons went to get falling-down drunk. There was a pile of junk behind the bar and a stand of pines.

Given the late hour, it wasn't long before a man came stumbling out of the bar, clearly three sheets to the wind. RJ stayed hidden in the dark behind one of the cars and waited until the man started to put his key into the door lock before he called to him.

"Harry?" RJ called, pretending to be drunk as he approached the man, the tire iron behind his back.

The man turned.

"Oh, sorry, I thought you were Harry Johnson." RJ was close now, close enough to smell the man's boozy breath.

"Nope, maybe he's still in the bar." The man turned back to his car, fumbling with the keys.

RJ hit him in the kidneys, then brought the tire iron down on the man's skull. He went down like a ton of bricks.

Unfortunately, the drunk was heavier than he looked, especially considering he was now dead weight. RJ dragged him behind the pile of junk and laid a scrap of sheet metal over him like a blanket.

He figured it would be a while before anyone found the guy and probably even longer before someone started searching for his vehicle.

Picking up the keys from the ground where the

man had dropped them, RJ opened the car door and climbed into the large older model American-made car. He swore. The man was a smoker, and the inside of the car reeked.

Well, beggars couldn't be choosers, as his father used to say. Just the thought of Ray Sr. made him grit his teeth. He wasn't the least bit sorry that old son of a bitch was dead.

RJ started the engine, turned on the radio, pulled away from the bar and headed for Whitehorse. Like the driver of the yellow Cadillac, he had the directions to the Winchester Ranch.

"It's out there and gone," the clerk had told him. "About as remote as it can get."

Josey didn't know it, but she'd chosen the perfect place to end this.

McCall WASN'T SURPRISED to hear from Detective Diaz in Palm City, California. She figured he was calling for an update, and while she had little in hard evidence, when she finished telling him what they had so far, he came to the same conclusions she had.

"That sounds like him," the detective said. "RJ skated on more than a few run-ins with the law, from breaking and entering, theft and assault to allegations from prostitutes who claimed he'd abused them. None of them ever made trial. I'm sure his father paid the people off."

McCall heard something in his voice. "And Josephine Vanderliner?"

"She went through a wild time when she was younger, nothing big. Speeding, drinking, a couple of marijuana possession charges, but she's been out of trouble since her mother's accident."

"What about Ray Sr.?"

"Nothing on the books, but he was living pretty high on the hog and running out of money fast when he married Ella Vanderliner."

"What about her car accident?"

Diaz chuckled. "Like minds. There was some question since it was a single car rollover. She had been drinking. The daughter was convinced it was foul play, saying her mother never had more than a glass of wine."

McCall could almost hear him shrug. "You said the mother is in a nursing home? Have you checked it to see if Josephine has called or stopped by?"

Diaz cleared his voice. "Actually, that's why I called. The mother was apparently moved, but the home swears they have no idea where."

"Someone had to sign her out."

"Apparently her daughter had made arrangements before…" His voice trailed off.

"Then she must have known she was going to come into some money," McCall said.

"It does give her more motive for killing Ray Sr.," Diaz agreed. "The battle she was waging in court was for control of her mother, which means control of her mother's money."

"Ray Sr. wouldn't have wanted that to happen."

"Nope," Diaz agreed. "But then neither would his son, RJ."

Chapter Eleven

On the way to the Winchester Ranch, Ray popped some of the pills he'd stolen and realized he felt better than he had in days. He could hardly feel his shoulder and he was thinking clearly, maybe more clearly than he ever had.

He'd realized how crucial it was to his plan that he found Josey. He wanted the money in that backpack, but more important he needed to make sure she never surfaced.

Once she was dead, he would inherit his father's money—which was the Vanderliner money. His father had been broke when he married Ella Vanderliner. It had been a godsend when she'd gotten into that car wreck and he'd gained control over all her money—including Josephine's, as luck would have it.

RJ laughed, wondering if his old man had planned it that way. Maybe the acorn hadn't fallen that far from the tree after all. But if that was the case, Ray Sr. had been holding out on him all these years.

Worse, he'd had to put up with this father's lectures every time he'd gotten in trouble when it was possible his old man was just like him. Hell, wouldn't it be something if he'd gotten his predilection for rough sex from

Ray Sr.? That would explain why his mother had taken off years ago and why his old man had paid to keep her in the style she'd become accustomed to, until she drowned in her fancy swimming pool.

RJ realized with a chill that his father might have been behind that accident, as well. But if true, then he really hadn't known his father at all.

He wheeled his train of thought back to his own problem: Josey Vanderliner. His fear now was that a judge would put Ella's care in Josey's hands. Unless Josey was arrested for murder, of course.

But RJ wasn't willing to put his life in the hands of a jury. He hated to think who would be more believable on the stand. That sweet-looking Josephine Vanderliner with the mother who was practically a vegetable. Or himself.

No, Josey had to disappear off the face of the earth. This was one body that could not be found.

Then he would surface and blame all of it on Josey. With her fingerprints on the weapon that had murdered his father, he didn't think he'd have that much trouble selling his story to the police. At least not in California.

It would be harder to explain the rest of what had happened. He thought he could sell the cops on a story that Josey had taken him and Celeste hostage. He had the bullet wound to prove that Josey had shot him. The rest he could say he didn't know anything about. He could say Josey had knocked him out and he came to underwater in the car. Let them try to prove he had anything to do with Celeste's death or that of the rancher.

Once he was cleared of any wrongdoing, he would be in charge of Josey's mother's care—and her money.

He'd put the old lady in the cheapest rest home he could find, one that cost even less than the one his old man had stuck her in. She wouldn't know the difference anyway.

"TALK TO ME, JOSEY," Jack said. He took her hand and led her over to the bed. As he sat down on the edge, he pulled her down next to him.

"I should never have involved you in this."

"It's too late for that," he said quietly. "You knew this woman they found, didn't you?"

Josey closed her eyes for a moment. "Her name was Celeste. I didn't know her last name. I'd never laid eyes on her before a few days ago."

Jack could feel Josey trembling and see the terror in her eyes, the same terror he'd seen the day he'd picked her up on the highway. He tried hard to hide his own fear as he asked, "Did you have anything to do with what happened to her?"

"No," she said with a shudder. "But I was there. I saw RJ unraveling. I saw it coming and I knew what he was capable of. I'd seen him…" Her voice broke.

"Why don't you start at the beginning."

She stared into his eyes for a long moment, then nodded slowly. He waited while she collected herself.

"You aren't going to believe me. I hardly believe it myself."

He squeezed her hand. "Don't worry. I'll know if you're lying."

She smiled at that. "You think you know me that well?"

"Yeah," he said simply. "I do."

Josey took a breath and let it out slowly. "I guess

it starts with my family. My father was Joseph Van-derliner."

Jack's eyebrows shot up. "*The* Joseph Vanderliner of Vanderliner Oil?"

She nodded. "That's the reaction I've been getting all of my life."

"I knew you came from money, just not that much money," he said. "I read that your father died a few years ago, and your mother..."

"She took my father's death hard. She was never a strong woman. I hadn't realized how weak she was until she married my stepfather, Ray Allan Evans Sr."

"You didn't like him."

"At first I thought he was all right. Until my mother had a car accident. The police said she'd been drinking, but she didn't like alcohol. She never had more than a glass of wine and usually not even that."

"This accident. Was your mother..."

"She survived, but she suffered massive head trauma. She will never recover." Her voice broke again. "Ray Sr. put her in a nursing home and took over her finances, which included my own. My father had died suddenly and hadn't updated his will, so my inheritance was still tied up with my mother's. I had a job at Vanderliner Oil, but when Ray Sr. took over he had me fired. I sued him, because I desperately needed to get my hands on my inheritance so I could take my mother out of that horrible rest home he'd stuck her in and get her proper care."

Josey rubbed a hand over her forehead. "My father's will was just ambiguous enough that my stepfather had control over not only all of my mother's and my money, but Vanderliner Oil, too. And he was spending the money as if there was no tomorrow."

She let go of his hand and stood up, pacing in front of the bed. "I should have been suspicious when my stepfather called and said he wanted to settle out of court, no lawyers. He had arranged, he said, to give me part of my inheritance as a show of faith. All I could think was that if I could get my hands on enough money I could help my mother. I should have known it was a trap."

McCALL HUNG UP from her call to Detective Diaz and heard the fax machine buzz. She walked down the hall and checked. Sure enough, it was the phone logs she'd been waiting for from Frank Hanover's house.

Her gaze went to the most recent calls, her heart starting to pound. There were five calls made during the time Frank said he and his wife had been in Billings.

All but one of the calls had been to Whitehorse, Montana numbers. McCall took the list back to her office, picked up the phone and dialed the out-of-state number first. A rest home? Hadn't Detective Diaz told her that Josephine's mother was in a rest home?

After she'd established that Ella had been in that rest home, she hung up, wondering why RJ had called there.

McCall dialed the first Whitehorse number.

"Packy's," a woman answered.

Why would RJ call a convenience mart?

McCall hung up and checked the other numbers. A call to the other two convenience marts in town. The rest were to motels in town.

She stared at the list. RJ was looking for someone.

She called the next number and recognized the woman's voice who answered at the hotel. "Nancy, it's McCall Winchester. Did you get a call from someone inquiring about a woman?"

Nancy Snider laughed. "Is this a crank call?" she joked.

"I have two missing persons, both considered armed and dangerous, and it seems one of them is searching for the other one. Help me out here. According to my phone log, the call would have come into the motel at eight-forty last night."

"Sorry. Now that you mention it, I did get a call last night."

"Man or woman calling?"

"Man. He asked if his girlfriend was staying here."

"Did he describe her?"

"Long, red-blond hair, curly, carrying nothing more than a backpack. Said they were supposed to meet up, but she got mad at him. Said he was worried about her."

"What did you tell him?"

"Said I hadn't seen her. Then he asked about some guy driving a yellow Cadillac convertible. Said she might be with him."

"A yellow Cadillac convertible?"

"Said it was one of those old ones with the big fins," Nancy said. "Told him I hadn't seen it, either."

But McCall had.

JOSEY CONTINUED TO PACE the bedroom, too nervous and upset to sit still. "When I got to the house, my stepfather was waiting. I could tell at once that he'd been drinking." She hesitated.

"He made a pass at you."

She laughed nervously. "How did you—"

"I know people."

"I slapped him. He became angry. I picked up a bronze statue he had on his desk in his library. He backed off and went to the wall safe, opened it and showed me the stacks of money—*my* money."

"How much money are we talking?"

"A little over a million in the safe," she said, and saw Jack's eyes widen.

"And the rest of your inheritance?"

She'd known he would realize she had more than that coming. "He had a letter releasing the rest of my inheritance to me. It was…sizable." She swallowed. "Ray said, 'Come get it, then get out.' I was wary. I said, 'Do you have something I can put it in?' He'd laughed and called out, 'RJ, get the lady something to put her money in.'"

"RJ," Jack repeated.

"Ray Allan Evans Jr." She swallowed again, her throat dry. "He appeared and I realized he'd been waiting in the next room."

Jack swore under his breath. "The two of them had set you up."

"RJ brought in an old backpack. It's the one I had when you picked me up on the highway. He tossed me the empty backpack and I moved to the safe just wanting to get the money and get out of there."

Jack listened, holding his breath.

"As I started loading the money into the backpack, I heard Ray Sr. order his son to get him a drink."

She took a breath and let it out slowly, remembering how everything had happened so fast after that. "I saw RJ. He had gone to the bar but he'd come back with only a bar rag. His father had taken a step toward me, saying something I didn't hear or just don't remember because of what happened next."

She was breathing hard now, the memory making her nauseous. "I had put the bronze statue back on Ray's desk. RJ walked past the desk, picked up the statue using the bar rag and struck his father in the back of the head. He hit him twice. I felt the spray of blood—" She was crying, remembering the way Ray Sr. had fallen at her feet.

Jack nodded as if he'd seen it coming. So why hadn't she? She'd known they were up to something, but she'd never dreamed...

"I must have been in shock. The rest is a blur. RJ was saying that his father never planned to let me leave with the money—or the legal document freeing up my inheritance. He shoved me aside. I was just standing there, staring down at Ray Sr. I could tell he wasn't breathing. The bronze statue was lying next to him covered with his blood. There was so much blood. RJ was frantically loading the money into the backpack. I saw it was splattered with Ray's blood."

"Let me guess. He wouldn't let you call the cops," Jack said.

"No. He said the only prints on the bronze statue were mine and that he would swear I'd killed his father for the money. Everyone knew about the legal battle I had been waging against my stepfather."

Jack swore. "They set you up and then he double-crossed his father."

Josey nodded. "I refused to go anywhere with him, but he pulled a gun and dragged me out of the house by gunpoint. When we got outside, he shoved me into the back of a car I had never seen before. That's when I saw that there was a woman in the car who'd been waiting for him."

"Celeste."

Josey nodded slowly. "She drove us to a secluded place while RJ held a gun on me. I thought they were going to kill me right there. I'd seen RJ kill his own father in cold blood. I knew he would shoot me without a moment's hesitation."

"Surely this Celeste woman—"

"She was excited, as if this was some great adventure. She didn't seem to notice the blood on RJ's clothing or that he had a gun. But he didn't kill me there. While he duct-taped my mouth, my wrists and ankles and shoved me into the trunk, she showed me the diamond ring RJ had bought her. He'd told her they were going to get married and then go on a long honeymoon."

"My God." Jack rose from the bed and took her in his arms.

"Oh, that was only the beginning," Josey said, as she leaned into his broad chest. "And now RJ is out there somewhere looking for me."

Chapter Twelve

RJ thought about taking a page out of Josey's playbook and drastically changing his appearance. But his last haircut and highlighting job had cost him a bundle and he wasn't about to ruin that with some disgusting dye job.

He decided he would just have to wear the farmer's straw hat to cover up most of his blond hair. His bigger concern was gasoline.

There was no way he could chance stopping at a station once he left Billings. There were only two towns between there and Whitehorse—Roundup and Grass Range, both small—and he'd heard on the radio that people were looking for him.

So he bought a gas can, put it in the trunk of the car he'd borrowed from behind the bar and filled it in Billings. Fortunately, the car had a large gas tank. The last thing he wanted to do was run out of gas before he found the Winchester Ranch.

His plan was to get to the ranch early enough that he could watch the comings and goings. He had no way of knowing how many people were on the place or how to find Josey. Once he had her, she would tell him where the backpack was with the money in it. At least the money better be in it, he thought.

There was always the chance that she wasn't even on the ranch anymore, but if the yellow Cadillac was there, then he would at least be able to find out where Josey had gone.

The drive was a lot longer than the clerk who'd given him the directions had led him to believe. This place was from hell and gone on miles of narrow dirt road. He was getting annoyed, the drugs he'd taken starting to wear off, when the right rear tire blew.

JACK COULD SEE how hard this was for Josey, but he had to know everything. It was the only way he was going to be able to help her. And no matter what she told him, he knew he would help her any way he could.

He'd never planned to let himself become emotionally involved with this woman, especially knowing from the get-go that she was in some kind of trouble.

But she'd brought out every protective instinct in him, and somewhere along the way he'd found himself falling for her.

"I realized he'd framed me for his father's murder, and the only reason he didn't dump me beside the road was because he needed to make it look as if I'd taken off with the money. I knew something else."

"He couldn't let you live," Jack said.

She nodded. "With his father dead and my mother unable to take care of herself, RJ would be in charge of everything my father had built. I knew he would destroy Vanderliner Oil, spend until he lost it. But I was more worried about what would happen to my mother.

"RJ was all drugged up, flying high, thinking he'd

just pulled off the perfect crime. I had no idea how far he'd driven before he stopped. I thought he was going to kill me then, but he just let me out long enough to go to the bathroom, give me some water and a little something to eat. Apparently, he didn't want me dying in his car and smelling it up."

"He didn't give you any idea where you were headed?"

Josey shook her head. "I asked him to let me ride in the backseat and promised I wouldn't cause any trouble. I wanted to know where we were. I also didn't stand a chance of getting away bound up in the trunk. With my wrists taped behind me, what could I do anyway?"

"So he agreed."

"I think he did it because he was already over Celeste," Josey said. "She was complaining about everything, especially about having to guard me whenever we stopped for gas or he had to run in and get food. At one point, she told him she wasn't going any farther unless he dumped me."

Jack shook his head in disbelief. "She was as cold-blooded as he was."

"The money was part of the appeal. At one point, they thought I was sleeping, and I heard him explain to her that he had to make sure no one found my body and that was why they were going to a place he and his father had hunted in Montana."

"You had to be terrified."

"I watched for an opportunity to get away, but as drugged up as RJ was, he never let down his guard. He seemed ultraintuitive to even the slightest movement by me. By the time we reached Montana I realized he was going to get rid of not only me, but also Celeste. Unfortunately, she hadn't figured that out yet."

McCall GOT THE CALL about a possible suspect sighting in Billings and hoped the recent incidents down there were RJ's doing only because it would mean he was nowhere near Whitehorse or the Winchester Ranch.

"We had a drugstore break-in," the cop on duty told her. "He sprayed something over the video camera, but missed a small spot. It was definitely a white male. Could be this Ray Allan Evans Jr. you're looking for."

"We believe he was injured at the scene and might be in need of medical supplies."

"Drugs and medical supplies were stolen. That same night a man was killed behind a bar and a pickup truck was set on fire near there. We also had a break-in at a house not far from the bar. A handgun was taken."

That sounded like her man. McCall made a note to see if Sharon Turnquist could get her the serial number on her husband's pickup. "What about the murdered man's car?"

"Missing." He rattled off the make and model and license plate number.

McCall was betting that RJ was now driving it.

After she hung up with the Billings police, she phoned the rest of the numbers that RJ had called. A few of the people who'd talked to him either hadn't come in yet for their shifts or had the day off. She asked for their numbers and tracked them down.

"Sure, I remember talking to him," the young male clerk at one of the motels told her. "He was trying to find his girlfriend. They'd gotten into a fight and she took off with some other guy. The guy did have a great car though. It was one of those Cadillacs with—"

"What kind of information did you give him?" McCall interrupted.

"Pretty much the same as the other guy—directions to the Winchester Ranch."

"The other guy?"

"The cowboy driving the Cadillac convertible. He was getting gas at Packy's the same time I was."

"Was he traveling alone?"

The clerk laughed. "The second guy asked me the same thing. I told him about the woman I saw with the cowboy. Didn't match the description he gave me of her, but he sounded like she was the one he was looking for."

Didn't match the description? "What did the woman look like?"

"Pretty with short, curly, dark hair."

The same way her grandmother had described Jack's wife, Josey.

Josey. Josephine. The moment McCall hung up, she dialed her grandmother's number at the ranch. The phone rang and rang. Her grandmother didn't have voice mail, but she had an old answering machine. When it didn't pick up, McCall realized there could be only one reason why.

The phone line was out.

In the middle of winter it wouldn't have been unusual for the phone line to be down. But this time of year?

It seemed odd. RJ could have reached the ranch by now, but would he cut the phone cord in broad daylight? It was more likely he would watch the place and hit it tonight.

Without cell phone service anywhere near the ranch, there was no way to reach her grandmother to warn her.

McCall feared it was too late to warn any of them as she jumped in her patrol car and, lights and siren blaring, headed for the Winchester Ranch.

RJ SHOULDN'T HAVE BEEN SURPRISED to find no spare tire in the trunk. He pulled out the tire iron and beat the trunk lid until it looked like the craters on the moon. He felt a little bit better after that.

Back in the car, he downed a half-dozen pills, then drove until there was no rubber left on the tire and the rim buried itself in a rut. The car wasn't going any farther, he thought with a curse, then realized it was blocking the road to the ranch. With an embankment on one side and a ravine on the other, no one would be coming down this road tonight.

He studied the directions he'd been given under the dome light. If he was right, he could cut off some of the distance by going across country. He drank the last of the twelve-pack he'd bought in Billings. It was hot and tasted like crap, but he didn't want to get dehydrated and it helped the buzz he had going.

There was just enough gas left in the can in the trunk to soak the front seat pretty good. He lit the car and, taking the map, dropped off the side of the road and headed what he believed was southwest. The night was cloudy, but earlier he'd seen the moon coming up in the east.

He heard the *whoosh* as the car caught fire, and he was glad there wasn't much gas in the tank. Even if the car did explode, though, he doubted the sound would carry clear to the ranch. He'd hate for them to have even an inkling of what was coming.

As he topped a rise, he realized he couldn't be that far from the ranch. Pleased that maybe things were turning out as they were supposed to for once, he counted the minutes before he'd see his stepsister again.

IT HAD GOTTEN DARK out. All Josey wanted to do was finish the story so Jack would understand why she had to get out of there. It was getting later, and the breeze coming in through the French doors was almost cold. She feared another storm was brewing on the horizon, and she worried about the road out of the ranch if there was a thunderstorm. She'd heard Enid say that when it rained here, parts of the road became impassable.

"When Celeste heard that we were going to camp, it was the last straw," she said. "We'd been eating fast food for thirty hours, sleeping in the car, and Celeste was ready for the good life RJ had been promising her. Also, he'd been popping a lot of pills so he could keep driving straight through, and he was acting oddly. When we reached the camp, RJ cut me free of the duct tape and tied me to a tree with part of the rope he'd brought along. I thought I might stand a chance since the rope was much less restricting than the tape.

"That night he and Celeste got into a huge argument. RJ demanded she give back the engagement ring. Celeste went ballistic and started hitting him. He grabbed her and tried to take the ring off her finger. The next thing, she was screaming that he'd broken her finger, howling with pain. He hit her and she went down."

Josey stepped to the open French doors to look out into the darkness for a moment, hugging herself against the cold, against the thought of RJ and what he was capable of. "He'd been playing with the extra rope he'd brought. But it wasn't until then that I saw he'd fashioned two lengths with nooses at the ends. RJ was saying something about Montana being the last of the old West. He tied one end of the rope to the bumper of the car, threw the other end over a limb near the water and looped the noose over Celeste's neck and pulled it tight. He abused her all the time. It seemed to be their thing, but this was different. Then he came for me saying it was time to hang the bitches."

She looked back at Jack and saw the pain and fury in his face before hurrying on. "I fought him, but he was too strong for me."

"That's how you got all the bruises."

Josey nodded. "I must have passed out because when I woke up, RJ was in the car, the motor running and I was being dragged by my throat. Celeste had come to and she was screaming for him to stop. He kept going in the car until we were both hauled off our feet and were hanging from the tree limb. I remember gasping for breath. Then I heard this huge crack as the limb broke, and the next thing I knew I was falling. The moment my feet hit the ground, I tore the noose from my neck.

"I had seen where RJ had laid down the gun when he was hitting me. I ran for it. I grabbed the pistol and spun around. Celeste still had the noose around her neck, but she'd found RJ's knife he'd used to cut the rope earlier. RJ saw her and hit the gas in the car. She sliced through the ropes before they went taut again."

Josey closed the French doors and stepped back into the room, still hugging herself against the memory— and the cold fear. "RJ threw the car into Reverse and headed right for her. I had the gun in my hand. I fired, but missed him, hitting the car instead. I fired again. I heard him cry out. I'll never forget the murderous look in his eye. Then he must have realized he was still in Reverse and headed for the river.

"It happened so fast. Celeste threw herself through the driver's-side open window. They were struggling as the car crashed into the river. Celeste had RJ in a headlock. RJ was wounded and trying to fight her off. Neither seemed to notice or care that the car was sinking. I grabbed the backpack and ran, still holding the gun.

"When I finally did stop on a rise to look back, I didn't see either of them. By then I'd realized that if I had any hope of getting my mother out of that awful place Ray Sr. had put her in, I couldn't turn myself in. At least not before I wired the money to the facility I'd set up for her the night I met Ray Sr. to pick up the money. Now all I have to do is make sure my mother is safe, then go to the police and—"

"RJ is still out there," Jack broke in. "It's going to be your word against his, and as you said, your fingerprints are on the murder weapon. If you turn yourself in, you'll go to prison—and what will happen to your mother?"

"I hid her. He won't be able to find her." But even as she said the words, she knew her mother wouldn't be safe.

"And what happens when this money you have runs out?"

Josey raked a hand through her hair. "Don't you think these are the things I've been trying to figure out?"

"I know," he said, taking her in his arms. "That's why

we need to figure them out together. I can finish what I came to do tonight and we can get out of here."

She pulled back to look into his face. "Jack—"

"We're in this together now. I just need you to trust me and stay in this room," he said. "We'll leave first thing in the morning. I know of a place we can go until we can make sure your mother was moved and is safe. Then—"

"You're planning on going after RJ," she said. The thought of Jack being in danger terrified her more than RJ coming after her alone. "No. I can't let you do that."

He cupped her shoulders in his hands. "We can talk about this later. I need to go. There is something I have to do. It's from a promise I made a long time ago. I feel I have to do this. Stay here. I'll try not to be long. Keep the door locked." He touched her cheek, a tenderness warming his blue eyes. "I'm not going to let anything happen to you. Get packed and wait for me. I'll hurry."

IT WAS DARK when McCall came around the corner in her patrol SUV, and her headlights flashed on the burned vehicle in the middle of the road. She pulled up, grabbed her flashlight and got out, half hoping to find RJ's body in the car.

Instead, she found footprints and tracked them a short distance in her flashlight beam. They were headed southeast toward the Winchester Ranch.

RJ had a good walk ahead of him. As she climbed back into her SUV, she could only hope he stumbled across a rattlesnake or broke his leg in a prairie dog hole. Backing up, she turned around and returned to the main road. Unlike RJ, she knew another way to get to the ranch that would be faster than walking. She considered calling for backup, but changed her mind. From the single set of footprints, RJ was alone. McCall figured he was after Josey Vanderliner, also known as Mrs. Jack Winchester.

The only thing McCall didn't know was how her cousin Jack fit into this.

RJ LET OUT a low whistle under his breath when the saw the Winchester Ranch. It looked like a damned hotel. Who were *these* people?

With a sinking feeling, he realized he was screwed if all those rooms were full of people. He'd never be able to find Josey—let alone get her out of there. Even with the gun he'd stolen in Billings, he couldn't take on everyone in the place.

He reminded himself he had no choice. Getting rid of Josey had become more than just something he needed to do to seal the deal on his father's death. It had become personal, he thought, as he rubbed his shoulder. If it wasn't for the pills he kept popping, he would be in horrible pain. As it was, his shoulder was a constant reminder of why he had to find Josey and finish this.

He moved down the hillside in the dark to the back of the massive log structure. Finding the main phone line coming in was child's play, since the pole was right behind the house. There was even a yard light nearby, so he wouldn't have to use the small penlight he'd brought.

But when he reached the spot where the phone line entered the house, he found that someone had already beat him to it. What the hell? The cord had definitely been cut. A sense of dread raced through his veins like ice water. Who would have done this?

Suddenly he wasn't so sure about finishing this here. Maybe he should just cut his losses, steal one of the cars, take some back road across the Canadian border. But he knew he wasn't going anywhere without money.

Still, this felt all wrong.

He moved around to the front of the place, staying in the shadows, the fine hairs on his neck standing on end. He came to a window with a light behind it and crouched down to listen.

He could hear a radio playing and someone banging around in the pots and pans and mumbling under her breath. He took a peek through the crack between the curtains. A small, elderly woman appeared to be cleaning up the kitchen in angry bursts.

RJ waited to see if anyone else showed up. When no one did, he moved along the edge of the house, staying to the dark shadow of the building.

He heard more voices, saw another lighted window, and eased forward. The window was open a crack, and he could hear two women talking.

"Give me a reason to stay here, Mother."

"Virginia, you have to do whatever it is you need to do."

"Can't you just say you want me to stay? Is that so hard for you? Or say you want me to leave. If it doesn't make any difference to you, that's the same as telling me to leave."

The older-sounding woman sighed deeply. "Why does everything with you have to be so dramatic? You've done nothing but complain since you got here. Why would you want to stay?"

RJ heard the younger one sniffle as if crying.

"Maybe I'd like to see my brothers and my nephews," she said, sounding hurt. "When are they arriving?"

"I don't know, Virginia. As you pointed out, they may not come to see me at all. I haven't heard from them. Or the rest of my grandchildren."

"I can't believe they won't."

"Perhaps they are less worried about their inheritance than you are," the older one said.

"You know, Mother, you deserve to die alone on this ranch with just Enid and Alfred here with you, both of them just waiting for you to breathe your last breath. I wouldn't be surprised if they helped that along one day."

He heard the scrape of a chair, then heavy footfalls and the slamming of a door. He listened but heard nothing more. Apparently, this place wasn't full. So far he'd only seen an old lady. But the daughter had mentioned two others, apparently caretakers.

As he started to move, he heard another sound, this one coming from outside the house. He pressed himself against the side of the house and stared out into the darkness.

Someone moved in the distance. Someone who seemed to be sneaking along the outside of the building—just as he had been doing.

The person who'd cut the phone line?

He waited until he saw the figure disappear inside a door at the far end of a separate wing of this monstrous place.

RJ waited for a moment, then followed.

IT DIDN'T TAKE Josey long to pack after Jack left, since she'd already started it earlier. She checked, though, to make sure she hadn't forgotten anything. Then she checked the gun she'd stuffed in the top of the backpack. She had only four bullets left. She hoped she wouldn't have to use them, but knew she would if they ran across RJ. As drugged up as he probably was, she wasn't sure it would be enough to stop him. The thought of killing him made her shudder. But she wouldn't let him hurt Jack, no matter what.

As she crossed in front of the French doors, she glanced out into the darkness, wondering where RJ was. Jack had said he wouldn't be able to find them on this ranch so far from everything. But Jack didn't know RJ.

Josey felt anxious, wishing Jack would hurry. They needed to get out of here, for their sakes and his grandmother's and Virginia's. She remembered Enid and Alfred. They seemed like they could take care of themselves.

She put the gun back into the top of the backpack and pulled the drawstring closed. Silently, she prayed that her mother had been moved to the new health-care facility and that RJ couldn't get his hands on her. That would be Josey's one weak spot, and RJ would capitalize on it if he thought of it.

With everything done, she turned out the lights and stepped to the window. She knew where Jack had gone. What she still didn't know was what was so important behind that rock wall. He'd said it was something he'd promised to do a long time ago. She knew Jack was the kind of man who stood by a promise no matter what.

What scared her was just that. He was risking his life and hers. So what was behind that rock wall? Hidden treasure? The famous Winchester fortune Jack had told her about?

No, she thought. Knowing Jack it was something much more important.

Standing on the balcony in the darkness and cold, Josey wondered when the exact moment was that she'd fallen in love with Jack Winchester. Had it been that first kiss in the Cadillac? Or when he held her while she cried on that high ridge during their horseback ride? Or was it when he'd taken her in his arms and carried her over to the bed? Sometime over the past few days she'd begun to realize she was no longer pretending. She felt like his wife.

With a start, Josey realized that she'd just seen something move along the edge of the far building—the same one Jack was in right now. It couldn't be Jack. He'd left a long time ago. Unless something—or someone—had held him up.

She stared hard into the blackness at the edge of the building, fear gnawing at her insides. If not Jack, then—

Alfred. The old man was sneaking along the edge of the building. He must have seen Jack go into the closed wing earlier. Or suspected that's where he was headed. What would Alfred do when he caught Jack opening that old rock wall? Why would he care?

She thought about the other night when Alfred had caught her in that wing. Had he gone back to make sure no one had tampered with the wall? Then that would mean he knew something had been hidden behind it.

Her heart began to pound.

What was he up to?

As he stepped to the edge of the far wing, the moon

slipped from behind the clouds. Her skin went clammy,
fear closing her throat, as she saw what Alfred gripped
in his hands. An ax.

Chapter Thirteen

Jack had made some progress on the rock wall the past two nights. He worked harder and faster tonight, anxious to get back to Josey. He didn't believe there was any way that her homicidal stepbrother could find her, and he'd made sure he had the Cadillac keys on him so she didn't do anything crazy like leave on her own.

He wished he could just let this go, but he'd promised his mother and himself years ago that he would see that Pepper Winchester got what she deserved. Today was that day. Then he could put this place and all that behind him.

But even as he thought it, Jack realized that something had changed in him. For years he'd been waiting for an opportunity to get back on this ranch and see what was behind this wall. It had always been there, that need to finish things in Montana. It hadn't mattered how well his life or his career had been going in Wyoming. There had always been this mission hanging over his head.

Now, though, his thoughts kept returning to Josey, and he realized just how much he'd changed since he'd met her. It was all he could do to keep chipping at the mortar. Did he really need to know what was behind this wall anymore?

The mortar in the wall was old, more than forty years. He chipped out another stone and set it aside. As he shone his flashlight into the space behind the wall, he could make out what looked like a large bundle wrapped in cloth.

His pulse kicked up a beat. Hurriedly, he removed another rock. There was definitely something in there. Something wrapped in what appeared to be an old canvas tarp.

For so long he hadn't been sure if his mother's story was even true. After all, she'd heard it from Angus Winchester, her lover, the man who'd lied to her for years.

Jack worked another rock out, and then another. Just a few more and he would be able to see what had been hidden for all these years behind this rock wall.

AFTER SEEING ALFRED with the ax headed for the wing where she knew Jack was working, Josey grabbed the gun out of the backpack and tore out of the room at a run. She heard someone call to her as she threw open the front door, but she didn't look back as she sprinted toward the closed wing.

The air chilled her to her bones. That and the fear that had her heart in her throat. There was no sign of Alfred as she ran the length of the building. She skidded to a stop as something moved out of the darkness just before she reached the door into the closed wing.

A low rumbling sound filled the air, and she froze as she saw the old dog. It blocked the way, the hair standing up on the back of its neck, a low growl coming out of its throat.

It took a step toward her. She raised the gun, but knew she wouldn't be able to shot it. "Nice dog," she whispered, and took a step away from it and the side of the building. The dog remained where it was. She took another step, then another, frowning. The old dog acted almost as if it was protecting something.

A bone? She squinted into the blackness at the edge of the building. Her blood suddenly ran cold. At first she thought it was a fawn deer or some other animal that the dog had killed and was only protecting its food.

But then she caught the glint of metal and saw that something was protruding out of the center of the dead animal. An ax.

"Oh, my God," she breathed as the moon broke free of the clouds, and she saw Alfred lying on his back, the ax buried in his chest.

Her mind whirled. Who would…? Jack! Where was Jack?

She turned and ran the last few steps to the door into the closed wing.

Jack removed the last rock in his way. Kneeling down, he picked up one end of the tarp. The canvas, rotten after all these years, disintegrated in his fingers.

The first thing he saw was what was left of a boot. He suddenly felt weak as he stared at what lay beyond the boot—a mummified body. Call Winchester.

Jack sat back on his haunches, surprised at the range of emotions that rushed through him like a wildfire. He'd dreamed of the day he would fulfill his promise to his mother. He'd expected revenge to taste sweet. Finally Pepper Winchester would get what she deserved.

But there was no sweetness, only a deep sorrow in him as he looked at what he knew were his grandfather's remains. He'd spent his adult life working hard to succeed in business, waiting for the opportunity to break down this wall and show the world who Pepper Winchester really was. It was going to make it all that much sweeter that she was still alive and would know who uncovered her deadly secret.

Jack waited for the relief, the elation, the smug satisfaction. He finally had proof that his grandmother had killed her husband and hidden his body behind this rock wall, just as his mother had heard.

He'd gotten what he'd come for. He didn't give a damn about any inheritance. Now all he had to do was call his cousin the sheriff and let her take it from here. He could wash his hands of this place that had haunted him all these years.

But what he hadn't expected was to feel a connection to this ranch or this family. He hadn't expected to meet Josey or fall in love. Or feel anything for his grandmother, let alone a dead grandfather he'd never known.

Jack heard a sound behind him. Josey, he thought. Of course she wouldn't be able to stay in the room. She would be worried about him. She would— He turned and saw the figure framed in the doorway.

PEPPER WINCHESTER had been coming out of the parlor when she'd seen Josey racing down the stairs as if the devil himself were after her.

"Call the sheriff," Josey had cried. "I have to get to Jack."

She'd tried to stop the girl to make sense of what was happening, but Josey had rushed out without answering.

The fear in the young woman's face had sent an arrow of panic through Pepper's own heart.

"What is wrong with that girl?" Virginia demanded, coming out from her room at the back wing.

"Stay here. Call the sheriff. Tell McCall there's some kind of trouble."

Her daughter's eyes widened in alarm. "You're not going out there."

But Pepper was already following Josey. She couldn't move as quickly, and once outside it took her a few minutes for her old eyes to adjust to the dark. She caught a glimpse of Josey running toward the closed wing of the lodge.

That building was actually the first homestead. Call had workers add on to it, the lodge expanding, as his grandiose plans developed, into what it was today. But Pepper remembered his stories about his parents living in what people would call an old shotgun house. Long and narrow, the hall ran straight through every room to the back door. Only this one didn't have a back door. The house ended in an old root cellar tucked into the hillside.

She saw Josey stop, heard the old dog growling even from here. As she worked her way in that direction, Pepper realized it had been years since she'd ventured out of the house. She wasn't used to walking on uneven ground, even with her cane. She felt exposed out here and suddenly afraid as she saw Josey give the dog a wide berth before slipping past the dog and disappearing into the door of the wing Pepper had Alfred close off years ago.

She quickened her pace, gasping for breath, as she

realized that what she had feared for more than forty years was about to come true.

RJ WAS MOVING down the hallway toward a scratching sound and a sliver of light under one of the doors, when he heard someone come into the house behind him. He quickly stepped into one of the darkened rooms, pressing his back against the wall.

He'd heard the dog growling, heard someone trying to soothe it. He'd expected whoever it was to run back to the house screaming after seeing the old man's body with the ax buried in it.

Rubbing his wounded shoulder, RJ swore under his breath at the pain. He hadn't seen the old man until it was too late. He'd sensed someone behind him in time to avoid the brunt of the ax. But the wooden handle had hit his shoulder.

The ax had stuck in the side of the log house. As the old fool had tried to wrestle it free, RJ had hit him, knocking him backward. Then, close to blacking out from the pain of the blow on his already injured shoulder, RJ had furiously jerked the ax from the wall and swung it as hard as he could. It stuck with a suctioning sound.

RJ had looked around, but he hadn't seen anyone else. *One down,* he'd thought. Then he'd heard an odd noise coming from within the building. He'd looked for a way into this wing and found an old door where someone had removed the boards that had been tacked over it.

Someone was in there working at this hour? There was a chipping sound, then a scraping sound, as if something large was being moved across the floor.

He'd opened the door, listened, then stepped through,

and was partway down the hall when he'd heard someone come in behind him.

Now he held his breath, wondering what was going on and why everyone was headed for this particular part of the strangely built house. The only light was a faint glow coming from under a door farther down the hallway. Where he stood there was total darkness. But he could feel a draft and realized that the window across from him, although partially boarded up, had a hole in the glass between the boards the size of a small rock.

Tentative footsteps moved in his direction. RJ pulled the gun he'd stolen from his jacket pocket, half wishing he'd brought the ax with him. He didn't dare fire the weapon for fear of who it might attract. He'd have to use it as a blunt force instrument. He'd had some experience with that.

As he listened to the footsteps growing closer and closer, he heard something outside the building that made his heart beat faster and his stomach drop. Through the broken window came the whine of a car engine in the distance.

It was headed toward the house, which meant there was another road into the ranch.

McCALL HAD TURNED OFF her lights and siren as soon as she'd gotten out of town; she hadn't needed them because of the lack of traffic. Now she stopped in a low spot and killed her headlights and engine. She reached for her shotgun. She was already wearing the Kevlar vest under her jacket and had her Glock in her holster. Both the shotgun and the pistol were loaded and ready to go.

Easing open the door, she slid out and started down

the road. Over the first rise, she saw the lodge sprawled against the mountainside. She could hear the wind in the cottonwoods as she neared the creek. The antique weather vane on the barn turned slowly.

She pulled up short as her eyes picked up movement in front of the house. Someone was walking toward the far wing. She heard the tap of a cane on the gravel. Her grandmother? Where was she going?

McCall began to run, hoping to hell her grandmother wasn't armed and would mistake her for a trespasser. But she wasn't about to call out and warn RJ that she was coming. She'd have to take her chances with her grandmother.

VIRGINIA PEERED OUT THE WINDOW, seeing nothing. Where had her mother gone? The old fool. Well, she wasn't going out there after Josey, who'd probably just had a spat with her husband. Newlyweds!

She looked around, wondering where Enid and Alfred were. They lived in the wing opposite the kitchen and laundry rooms. Virginia realized she hadn't heard a peep out of either of them.

And it certainly wasn't like Enid to miss anything. Why hadn't she come out when Josey had come tearing through the house and both Virginia and her mother had raised their voices to call after her?

Virginia thought the whole thing ridiculous, but she stepped to the phone and began to dial 911 before she realized the line was dead.

She slowly put down the receiver. Her cell was useless out here; in fact, her grandmother didn't even own one and with good reason. Cell phone coverage was sketchy in this part of the county.

The huge old place seemed too quiet. She shivered and hugged herself, wishing her mother would come back and assure her there was a good reason the phone line was down.

Should she stay in here and wait, or should she go out and see what was going on herself? Maybe her mother needed her.

The thought actually made Virginia laugh out loud.

The wind buffeted the old glass at the window, making her jump. She'd been so busy listening to the house that she'd failed to realize how hard the wind was blowing. It thrashed the cottonwoods outside, sending leaves swirling across the yard.

She tried to convince herself that the wind had knocked down the phone line, just as it used to when she lived here. But she knew something was terribly wrong. She could feel it.

She eased open the front door and peered around the corner, hoping to see her mother. A gust of wind nearly wrested the door from her hands. She stared into the darkness. Was that Pepper headed for the old wing of the house?

She let out a small cry as ice-cold fingers bit into her upper arm. The door slipped from her fingers and swung open, banging against the wall as she swung around.

"What are you doing?" Enid demanded.

The elderly housekeeper looked odd. Or maybe it was the way the wind blew her hair back from her face in this dim light.

"You scared me half to death," Virginia snapped. "You have to quit sneaking up on people like that. You're going to give my mother a heart attack."

"It would take more than that to kill your mother."

Enid glanced down the hallway in the direction of Pepper's room. "Where *is* your mother?"

"She's gone outside after Josey."

Enid pushed past her, fighting the wind to see.

Virginia heard her mother scream like a wounded animal, the sound getting caught up in the howl of the wind, as Enid began to run awkwardly in the direction Pepper had gone.

Virginia slammed the door, then hurried down to her room and locked herself inside.

RJ KNEW HE COULDN'T BE SEEN where he was standing in dense shadow, and yet he'd almost blown it—he'd been so surprised to see Josey walk past the room where he was hiding in plain sight.

He wanted to laugh. Could his luck get any better than this? He felt he was on a roll. Nothing could go wrong.

The hardest part was waiting until he heard her footsteps stop. Still, he waited as he heard a door creak open. He started to take a step when he heard Josey speak—and a man answer.

Perfect. RJ took a cautious step out, then another. The door to the room down the hall was open now, a dim light spilling out. He could hear their voices, but couldn't make out what they were saying. Something in the tone, though, told him this was the driver of the Cadillac parked out front, the cowboy who'd saved Josey. Or thought he had, RJ thought with a smile.

He eased down the hallway, stopping as soon as he could hear what they were saying.

PEPPER TEETERED on her cane as McCall reached her.

"What is going on?" Pepper demanded, her voice warbling with emotion.

McCall steadied her for a moment, following her grandmother's gaze to the body lying in the shadow of the house and the old dog sitting next to it.

"It's Alfred," her grandmother said. "He has an ax in his chest."

McCall could see that. "What are you doing out here?"

"Josey rushed out of the house saying to call you because Jack was in trouble. I came out to find out what was wrong."

Josey, McCall thought, looking around the ranch yard. "I want you to go back to the house." At the sound of a sole crunching on the gravel, McCall swung around to see Enid. She had stopped short of where her husband lay dead next to the door. She had her hand over her mouth.

"Enid," McCall said, going over and taking hold of her arm. "I want you to take Pepper back into the house. Do you hear me?"

The ancient housekeeper nodded slowly.

"Now! Both of you, and stay there." McCall moved along the building, glancing back to see that neither old woman had moved. Damn it. She didn't have time to herd them back to the house. She reached the end of the building and saw where the boards had been removed.

The door into the old section of the house was open. Cautiously, she moved toward it.

FOR A MOMENT, Josey stood, her heart in her throat, afraid to breathe.

"Jack?" she whispered, as she stared into the dark room. The gun was in her hands, one finger on the trigger. She knew RJ might have already gotten to Jack. That if anyone was in the room it could be RJ, standing in the dark and laughing at her.

A light flashed on, the beam pointed at the floor.

Her finger brushed the trigger and jerked away. "Jack!" she cried. She lowered the gun and rushed to him. Her relief at seeing him unharmed made her throat swell with emotion. She could barely get the words out. "Alfred. He's dead. RJ—" The rest was choked off as she saw the hole in the wall and what lay just inside it. "Oh, my God. Who—?"

"My grandfather," he said, taking the gun from her and laying the flashlight on one of the shelves so the beam wasn't pointed at them. "My mother had heard stories from people who used to work on the ranch about Alfred rocking up a wall in the old wing the day Call Winchester disappeared."

The mention of Alfred brought back the horrible scene just outside. The words spilled out of her as she felt the urgency return. "I saw Alfred earlier carrying an ax and headed this way, so I came to warn you, but…" She shuddered as she met Jack's eyes. "He's dead. The ax is in…his chest. RJ's here."

Jack gripped her arm with one hand. He had the gun he'd taken from her in the other. "Come on, let's get out of here."

They both seemed to hear the creak of a floorboard behind them at the same time. Turning toward the doorway, Jack stepped in front of her as they were suddenly blinded by a bright light.

JACK BLINKED, covering his eyes as he shielded Josey from the man standing in the doorway holding the gun on them.

"Drop the gun," the man ordered, and lowered the flashlight so it wasn't blinding Jack.

Jack knew he could get off at least one shot before RJ fired. He couldn't take the chance that Josey might be hit.

He had risked her life for revenge. He would never forgive himself. But he knew even if they'd left earlier, one day RJ would have caught up to them. This encounter had been inevitable.

Jack just would have liked to be more prepared.

He felt Josey behind him, heard the small sound she made and knew this was indeed her stepbrother, RJ Evans, the man who'd framed her, hurt her and planned to kill her.

In the diffused light from the flashlight in his hand, Jack saw that RJ was tall and blond, with eerie blue eyes. He looked strong and solid and armed. Jack had to believe that RJ wouldn't want to kill them here in this room, that he would get an opportunity to save Josey. It couldn't end like this. He would do anything to save Josey.

"I said drop the gun. Now!"

Jack dropped the gun to the floor at his feet.

RJ smiled. "Hey, Josey. Shocked to see me? I thought you might be surprised that you hadn't killed me." He sounded angry, his words slurring a little as if he might be drunk or on drugs. "Could you have hidden someplace more hard to get to?" His gaze shifted to Jack. "And you must be the guy with the Cadillac convertible. Nice ride. I think I'll take it when I leave here."

Behind him, Jack felt something hard and cold suddenly pushed against his back. The crowbar. Josey slipped it into the waistband of his jeans.

"Now kick the gun over here," RJ ordered.

JOSEY KNEW how this would end. She knew what RJ was capable of, his cruelty unmatched. He would make them both pay, Jack for helping her and putting RJ to all this trouble, and Josey—

She couldn't think about that or the fear would paralyze her. This had to end here. The last time she'd shot at RJ it had been to stop him from killing both her and Celeste. She'd sworn then that she would never fire another gun, especially at another person.

RJ stepped forward before Jack could kick the gun over to him in a swift movement that caught both her and Jack by surprise. He caught Jack in the side of the head with the butt of his weapon.

Jack started to go down and Josey saw her chance. She dropped to the floor, snatched up the gun Jack had dropped and fired blindly at RJ. The gunshots exploded in the small room, deafening her, as she saw RJ stumble backward toward the doorway. His flashlight clattered to the floor and went out, pitching the room in blackness.

The air had filled with five shots. Josey knew she'd had only four in the gun she was holding. That meant RJ had gotten a round off. Her heart leaped into her throat at the thought that Jack might have been hit. If the blow to the head from the butt of the gun hadn't killed him, then the shot could have.

"Jack?" For a moment, the silence was deafening. Then a chill skittered over her skin as she heard RJ chuckle. He knew there had only been six shots in the pistol. He knew she was no longer armed.

She could hear him feeling around in the dark for something. His gun? Had he lost it? Then her heart began to pound wildly as she heard him crawling toward her. "Jack?" No answer.

She was filled with agony and terror that Jack was dead. Her plan had backfired. Somehow Jack had gotten in the line of fire.

She scuttled backward from her sitting position on the floor until she hit the rock wall. Her fingers felt rocks and dried mortar. She felt around frantically for a rock small enough that she could use as a weapon, but found nothing.

Remembering the hole Jack had made in the wall, she felt around for it, thinking that if she could get through it—

As she tried to scramble to her feet, disoriented by the blackness, RJ's hand closed like a vise around her ankle. She screamed, grabbing a handful of dried mortar from the floor and throwing it where she thought his face should be.

He let out a scream of his own, clawing at her now with both hands as she tried to fight him off. But RJ had always been too strong for her.

MCCALL HAD JUST STEPPED through the doorway and had started down the hall when she heard the five shots. She snapped on her flashlight. With her weapon drawn, she hurried down the hall.

She couldn't tell where the shots had come from. The sound had echoed through the wing. So she was forced to stop at each door, before moving forward again.

Behind her she heard a door open and spun around to see her grandmother standing in it, wide-eyed. Damn the stubborn woman. Hiding behind her was Enid.

McCall couldn't take the time to argue with them. She waved for them to stay back, knowing the effort was useless, as she moved forward down the hallway.

She hadn't gone far when the hallway light switched on. She swore. Her grandmother or Enid had just alerted whoever had fired those shots that they were no longer alone.

IN THE SUDDEN LIGHT, Josey saw that at least some of the four shots she'd fired had hit their mark. RJ had left a wide smear of blood on the floor as he'd crawled after her. He had pulled himself up into a sitting position and managed to get hold of her wrist, twisting it until she was sure he was going to break it, then pulled her facedown in front of him.

But when the lights had come on, her gaze had gone instantly to where she'd heard Jack fall. He lay just feet away. His eyes were closed and she could see that his shirt was soaked with blood. She stared at his chest, praying to see the rise and fall of his breath.

Please, God, let him be alive.

RJ let go of her wrist to grab a handful of her hair. He jerked her head up and slapped her almost senseless. "I'm talking to you, bitch. Look at me when I talk to you. I want you to be gazing into my eyes when I rip your heart out."

He'd already ripped her heart out if he'd killed Jack. She had fought RJ until he'd gotten her down on the floor. His face was scratched where she'd made contact, his eyes red and running tears, his cheeks gritty with mortar. He kept blinking and swearing as he tried to clear them.

But it was the way the front of his shirt blossomed with blood that gave her hope. "You're in no shape to rip my heart out," she said, meeting his gaze. She would fight this bastard to the death. "You're going to bleed to death on this dirty floor."

He laughed, a gurgling sound coming from his throat, that even gave him pause. A new cruelty came into his eyes. He wasn't going to die alone, the look said. He let go of her long enough to pull the knife from the sheath strapped to his leg.

Out of the corner of her eye, Josey caught movement. She wanted to cry in relief. She wanted to look in Jack's direction to make sure she hadn't just imagined it. But she did neither. She kept her gaze locked with RJ's, afraid of what he would do if he knew that Jack was alive.

Josey didn't move, didn't breathe, as RJ put the knife to her throat.

JACK CAME TO SLOWLY. The blow to his head had knocked him senseless. He lay perfectly still, listening to RJ threatening Josey. It was all he could do not to leap up and attack the man.

But first he had to be sure that RJ wasn't still holding a gun on her.

He moved his head as quietly as he could until he could see RJ sitting, leaning against the stack of rocks Jack had removed from the wall. He was turned slightly, so he wasn't facing Jack, but he didn't have his back to him, either.

Jack saw that RJ's shirt was soaked with blood. There

was a wide trail of blood on the floor where it appeared RJ had crawled over to Josey. He now had hold of Josey's hair and was holding her in front of him at an odd angle.

The last thing Jack remembered was the sound of gunfire. At first he'd thought RJ had unloaded his weapon on Josey. But now he could see Josey's gun lying within her reach. He could only assume it was empty or RJ would have taken it from her. She didn't appear to be wounded, but Jack couldn't know that for sure until he got a better look at her.

Shifting just a little, he felt the crowbar at his back and eased it out behind him. He knew he would get only one chance if RJ was still armed. He would have to make it count.

"You know, RJ, you might have pulled it off," Josey was saying. Jack realized she was stalling, giving him time. "The way you set me up when you killed your father, that was brilliant."

"Thanks." RJ sounded touched that she thought so. "I hated that mean old son of a bitch. I don't know why I didn't kill him sooner."

Jack heard something in RJ's voice and the way he was trying to catch his breath. He was bleeding badly and Jack suspected Josey had nicked a lung.

"Where you went wrong was taking Celeste along with you."

"Tell me," RJ agreed, struggling with each breath.

Josey had to have heard it, as well. She would be thinking that if she kept him talking...

Slowly, methodically, trying not to make a sound, Jack worked his way to a crouch. RJ's threats covered most any noise Jack had made.

"She was only after your money," Josey said. "I think you're better off without her."

"Uh-huh," RJ agreed. "You aren't going to suggest that I hook up with you, are you?" His laugh sounded as if he was underwater. "A woman who shot me not once, but twice?"

It wasn't until Jack was ready, the crowbar in his hand, that he saw a glint of metal and realized what RJ was holding to Josey's neck.

MCCALL HEARD VOICES and followed the low rumble down the hallway, then stopped just outside the room. She heard a man's voice, threatening to kill someone. Not her cousin Jack's voice. RJ's? She could only assume so.

Then she heard a woman's voice, scared, but in control. Josey Vanderliner? Where was Jack? Hadn't her grandmother said something about Josey going after Jack?

Leading with the weapon, McCall swept it across the room, taking in the scene and making a decision in that split second.

She'd heard everything said within the room and knew that RJ had some kind of weapon in his possession and planned to kill Josey. He sounded bad, but she knew that some men, especially those that took certain drugs, didn't die easily.

When she saw the knife RJ was holding to Josey's throat and her cousin Jack armed with a crowbar and ready to risk his life for this woman he called his wife, McCall didn't hesitate. She pulled the trigger.

Chapter Fourteen

It was chaos after that. Jack lunged forward even as RJ fell away from Josey, the shot to his head killing him instantly. Jack lunged, knocking the knife away from Josey's throat with the crowbar in the same instant McCall fired.

McCall heard her grandmother and Enid behind her. Heard the gasps. Jack was cradling Josey in his arms. Past them, McCall saw the hole in the rock wall and what appeared to be a mummified body lying in what was left of an old canvas tarp.

"It's Call Winchester," Enid cried. "Just like Alfred said."

McCall rounded up everyone and got them all back to the house, but not before she'd seen the expression on her grandmother's face as she looked at the mummified body behind the wall.

"I'm going to need statements from all of you," McCall announced after going to her patrol car and calling for backup, an ambulance and a coroner. "Starting with you. I assume you are Josey Vanderliner?"

Josey nodded.

"The rest of you just sit here quietly."

She took Josey down the hall to the first room McCall

had ever seen in this house just a month ago. It had taken a while, but her grandmother had accepted her as a Winchester.

Now, though, McCall was wondering if that was such a good thing, as she turned on the small tape recorder she'd retrieved from the patrol SUV.

"Tell me what happened here tonight," she said to Josey, and listened to the horrific story the young woman told, beginning with the murder of Ray Allan Evans Sr. in Palm City, California, and finishing with RJ holding a knife to her throat.

"I heard him confess to the murder of his father," McCall said, when Josey finished.

"Jack didn't know anything."

McCall smiled, thinking that her cousin was a Winchester. He knew something was up with this woman he'd picked up on the road. He'd helped her disguise her looks and given her a place to hide out. But she kept those thoughts to herself, secretly admiring Jack. There would be no charges of harboring a criminal since Josey Vanderliner had been a victim herself.

After that, McCall talked to Jack. "You knew there was a body behind that rock wall?"

"I thought it might just be a rumor."

She nodded. "Do you believe Enid that her husband, Alfred, killed Call Winchester?"

Jack grinned. Even though he was blond and blue-eyed, McCall saw the Winchester shining through. "I would have no idea."

She laughed, shaking her head. "The old gal got to you, too."

"I don't know what you're talking about," Jack said.

Enid repeated the same story she'd told on the way

to the house, swearing that Alfred had killed Call and that the only reason she'd kept silent all these years was that Alfred had threatened to kill her, as well.

McCall didn't believe a word of it.

Her grandmother looked pale by the time she came into the room. She sat down heavily, still holding her cane, appearing a little dazed.

"You must have wondered what happened to your husband," McCall said to her grandmother.

Pepper looked up, her eyes misting over. "I loved your grandfather. But it was a relief not to ever have to see him again because I *did* love him, and being around him hurt so badly, loving and hating him at the same time."

McCall was surprised at her grandmother's honesty. "What did you think happened to him?"

"You know this country. I thought eventually we'd find his body. I also thought he might have just taken off, put this life behind him. Your grandfather, well, he'd had other lives before I met him. I never knew where he got his money or how. But I did know that he liked the idea of reinventing himself. But to see him behind that wall…" Her voice broke. "Will the coroner be able to tell how he died?"

The question made the hair stand up on the back of her neck. "Probably not," McCall said slowly.

"I know what you're thinking, but I couldn't do that to him. I couldn't wall him up like that. Call was afraid of small spaces." She shuddered and wiped her eyes.

As McCall shut off the tape recorder, she didn't know if she believed her grandmother or not, but she wanted to.

JACK SANK DOWN into the bubbles, the water as warm and soothing as the feel of Josey's body tucked in front of him in the big clawfoot tub.

He pressed his face against hers, breathing in her scent, thanking God that she was all right.

They hadn't said much since McCall had allowed them to come upstairs and clean up. Their clothing would be taken as evidence, but since the acting sheriff had witnessed what had happened and had heard RJ confess to his father's murder, they had both been cleared.

"I thought I'd lost you," Jack said.

Josey cupped his face in her hands, her gaze taking him in as if memorizing every feature. "You aren't the only one. I was so worried that if the blow to the head didn't kill you then the one shot RJ got off did." There were tears in her eyes.

"You realize I'm not going to let you go."

She smiled almost ruefully. "Jack, we're virtually strangers."

"After what we've been through?" he scoffed, as he pulled her to him. "And we could have years to get to know each other better if you would say you'll really be my wife. I know this isn't much of a proposal—"

She touched her fingers to his lips. "This is the second best proposal I've ever had. The first was a few days ago on the highway."

He kissed her fingers, then removed them from his lips. "Well? Willing to take a chance with me?"

"One question. What is the Galaxy Corporation?" She looked chagrined. "I checked the registration in your car after you kept sneaking off in the middle of the night."

"It's a business I started that puts kids together with ranches. Oftentimes the kids are from the inner city or have been in trouble. I twist the arms of rich landowners, people who own large amounts of land but spend only a week or two actually at the ranch, to let the kids come work the place. Most ranch managers are fine with it as long as the kids are supervised. You can't believe what hard work and fresh air does for these kids."

She heard the love in his words for both ranching and kids. She should have known the Galaxy Corporation was something like that. "Did I mention how much I love you?"

"No." But his grin said he liked it. "I should tell you, though, I don't make any money doing this. Fortunately, it turns out that my mother's family had money. That helped get the corporation going so that now it is self-supporting."

Josey laughed. "I have a ton of money, more than I will ever spend. What?" she said, when she saw his expression.

"I don't like the idea of marrying someone who—"

"Can expand your kids-on-ranches program?" she asked.

He smiled at her. "Still—"

"The answer is yes. If you still want to marry me."

He looked into her beautiful green eyes and felt his heart soar like a hawk. "I don't want to spend another day away from you."

"You won't have to. My mother is safe. McCall checked for me. I will want to move her closer to wherever I'm going to be, that's all I need. Well, maybe not *all* I need." Desire sparked in her gaze. "I need you, Jack Winchester."

They made love in the tub, slowly, lovingly, a celebration of life. It wasn't until they were drying off that Jack broached the subject.

"My grandmother has asked me if I'd like to come back to the ranch at some point. I told her I would have to talk to you. I think everything that has happened has changed her. Well, at least a little. I know you probably have nothing but bad memories here and there is more than a good chance that my grandmother had something to do with my grandfather being put behind that stone wall, you know."

"Jack, you love this place and I love you."

"But after everything that's happened, not to mention the secrets that these walls have seen…"

She stepped to him, wondering at how fate and maybe a whole lot of luck had brought Jack Winchester into her life. She wanted to pinch herself. "I will be happy wherever you are."

He grinned as he reached for her, drawing her back into his arms. "I was thinking we should elope and go on a long honeymoon, then if you still mean it, maybe we'll come back here for McCall's wedding at Christmas and see how things go."

Josey kissed him, remembering that day on the highway when he'd come roaring up the hill in his old Cadillac convertible and had stopped for her. She remembered his handsome face beneath the brim of his Western hat. But what she remembered most was that boyish grin of his.

"Pepper said she would give me a section of land so we could build a house of our own," Jack said between kisses, as he carried her over to the bed. "We'll need lots of room for all those kids we're going to have together. I'm thinking a half dozen."

Josey laughed as he lowered her to the bed. She pulled him down. "It is definitely something we can negotiate," she said.

"I love you, Josey," Jack said, grinning. "Taking you for a wife was the smartest thing I ever did."

* * * * *

Harlequin offers a romance for every mood!
See below for a sneak peek from
our suspense romance line
Silhouette® Romantic Suspense.
Introducing HER HERO IN HIDING by
New York Times *bestselling author Rachel Lee.*

Kay Young returned to woozy consciousness to find that she was lying on a soft sofa beneath a heap of quilts near a cheerfully burning fire. When she tried to move, however, everything hurt, and she groaned.

At once she heard a sound, then a stranger with a hard, harsh face was squatting beside her. "Shh," he said softly. "You're safe here. I promise."

"I have to go," she said weakly, struggling against pain. "He'll find me. He can't find me."

"Easy, lady," he said quietly. "You're hurt. No one's going to find you here."

"He will," she said desperately, terror clutching at her insides. "He always finds me!"

"Easy," he said again. "There's a blizzard outside. No one's getting here tonight, not even the doctor. I know, because I tried."

"Doctor? I don't need a doctor! I've got to get away."

"There's nowhere to go tonight," he said levelly. "And if I thought you could stand, I'd take you to a window and show you."

But even as she tried once more to pull away the quilts, she remembered something else: this man had been gentle when he'd found her beside the road, even when she had kicked and clawed. He hadn't hurt her.

Terror receded just a bit. She looked at him and detected signs of true concern there.

The terror eased another notch and she let her head sag on the pillow. "He always finds me," she whispered.

"Not here. Not tonight. That much I can guarantee."

Will Kay's mysterious rescuer protect
her from her worst fears?
Find out in HER HERO IN HIDING
by New York Times bestselling author Rachel Lee.
Available June 2010, only from
Silhouette® Romantic Suspense.

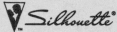

LARGER-PRINT BOOKS!

GET 2 FREE LARGER-PRINT NOVELS

PLUS 2 FREE GIFTS!

HARLEQUIN®
INTRIGUE®

Breathtaking Romantic Suspense

HILP10R

HARLEQUIN®

Showcase

On sale May 11, 2010

Reader favorites from the most talented voices in romance

Save $1.00 on the purchase of 1 or more Harlequin® Showcase books.

SAVE $1.00 on the purchase of 1 or more Harlequin® Showcase books.

Coupon expires Oct 31, 2010. Redeemable at participating retail outlets. Limit one coupon per purchase. Valid in the U.S.A. and Canada only.

52609015

Canadian Retailers: Harlequin Enterprises Limited will pay the face value of this coupon plus 10.25¢ if submitted by customer for this product only. Any other use constitutes fraud. Coupon is nonassignable. Void if taxed, prohibited or restricted by law. Consumer must pay any government taxes. Void if copied. Nielsen Clearing House ("NCH") customers submit coupons and proof of sales to Harlequin Enterprises Limited, P.O. Box 3000, Saint John, NB E2L 4L3, Canada. Non-NCH retailer—for reimbursement submit coupons and proof of sales directly to Harlequin Enterprises Limited, Retail Marketing Department, 225 Duncan Mill Rd., Don Mills, ON M3B 3K9, Canada.

U.S. Retailers: Harlequin Enterprises Limited will pay the face value of this coupon plus 8¢ if submitted by customer for this product only. Any other use constitutes fraud. Coupon is nonassignable. Void if taxed, prohibited or restricted by law. Consumer must pay any government taxes. Void if copied. For reimbursement submit coupons and proof of sales directly to Harlequin Enterprises Limited, P.O. Box 880478, El Paso, TX 88588-0478, U.S.A. Cash value 1/100 cents.

5 65373 00076 2   (8100)0 11651

® and TM are trademarks owned and used by the trademark owner and/or its licensee.
© 2009 Harlequin Enterprises Limited

HSCCOUP0410

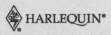 HARLEQUIN®

INTRIGUE®

COMING NEXT MONTH

Available June 8, 2010

#1209 THE BABY'S BODYGUARD
Bodyguard of the Month
Alice Sharpe

#1210 TWELVE-GAUGE GUARDIAN
Whitehorse, Montana: Winchester Ranch
B.J. Daniels

#1211 DADDY DEVASTATING
Texas Maternity: Hostages
Delores Fossen

#1212 ROYAL CAPTIVE
Defending the Crown
Dana Marton

#1213 MYSTERY LOVER
Shivers
Lisa Childs

#1214 NIGHT MOVES
Thriller
HelenKay Dimon

HICNMBPA0510